# *Wilhelmina*

## A WINTER BRIDE

MAIL ORDER BRIDES FOR ALL SEASONS

# HILDIE McQUEEN

PINK DOOR PUBLISHING • 2017

Wilhelmina, a Winter Bride
MAIL ORDER BRIDES FOR ALL SEASONS

Copyright © Hildie McQueen 2017

Pink Door Publishing
Augusta, Georgia

Editor: Scott Moreland
Cover Artist: Dar Albert
Interior Formatting: Author E.M.S.

ISBN-13: 978-1-939356-57-4

Published in the United States of America

# Chapter One

*Philadelphia, Pennsylvania 1872*

The carriage rocked side to side as Wilhelmina Wilkins and her family rode to the first ball of proper society's winter season. It was not as enchanting an evening as one would think. Wilhelmina let out a sigh, wishing to be back home in the privacy of her bedroom and not having to share space with her stepmother and stepsister.

As usual, her father managed to keep a measured distance although occupying the same cramped space. If there were a trait she wished to get from him, it would have to be the ability to not be so present in every moment.

Her lips curved at noting his eyes swept the interior of the carriage and then quickly turned back to the book he held. Dim as it was in the carriage, he could not make out a single word, of that Wilhelmina was sure. However, the act of pretending to read did deliver the perfect silent statement of not wanting to be disturbed.

"Now Wilhelmina, ensure that you keep a distance between yourself and Gilda. She has to make an entrance."

Laverne Wilkins' narrowed eyes met Wilhelmina's over the ever-present fan in her hand.

Wilhelmina's stepmother continued, "It is her coming out night after all."

Why it was Gilda's night again wasn't exactly clear to Wilhelmina. But since she couldn't care less, all she gave the woman seated across the plush carriage was a one-shouldered shrug. "Of course. I wouldn't dream of taking attention away from Gilda."

Her stepsister and stepmother exchanged looks, the disdain for Wilhelmina obvious. "Yes, well, ensure you remain behind me," Laverne finished then peered out the carriage window. "Oh look, Gilda! How grand the Jamesons' house looks tonight."

Despite her sour mood, Wilhelmina looked out and, indeed, the great mansion was splendid. Lanterns swung from low tree branches and paper banners flew in the cool breeze. The first of many balls of the winter season meant the hosts would put every effort into setting the bar high.

The Jamesons were an established Philadelphia family, the elite class, which only old money could attain.

Every year since she could remember, their party was the one to attend. The members of their social circle held their breaths waiting for an invitation to the affair.

The patriarch, Milford Jameson III, was heir to millions and his wife, Pearl Worthington Jameson, had a pedigree to match. They had one married daughter and two sons, both deemed to be the most eligible bachelors in the state. Every family hoped their daughters would catch the eye of Milford, the eldest son, or Ernest, the second born. Neither appealed to Wilhelmina since both were known rakes.

Ernest, the more handsome of the two, was a devilish rogue. And Milford, the first born, was well known for his affinity for visiting houses of ill repute. It was whispered both tended to enjoy rather dark tastes when it came to the bedroom. That alone should warn the overanxious parents off in Wilhelmina's estimation.

Wilhelmina had met both and cared for neither. What she looked most forward to this night was seeing her childhood friend, Aurora, with whom she could spend time people watching and discussing what everyone wore. The new debutantes would keep them entertained with their antics at attempting to get the attention of the single men present.

Neither she nor Aurora aspired to marriage. Not for some time yet and both held on to the notion that when they did marry, it would be when falling desperately in love with an astonishingly handsome man. Their future husbands would be honorable men who would concede to their every whim.

The thought brought a chuckle, earning her a glare from her stepmother.

The carriage came to a stop but no one moved. The procession of carriages meant it would be a while yet before they arrived at the front of the house and be assisted by footmen to descend.

Gilda leaned over her mother in an attempt to look out. "Do you see anyone of interest mother?"

Laverne leaned out to look with a delighted smile. "The Penningtons are about to enter. Oh my. Mary is wearing a dress in the most dreadful shade of green. Goodness, I can't believe her seamstress didn't warn her it is most definitely not her color."

Wilhelmina looked in the direction of the entrance and had to agree with her stepmother for once.

Finally, they arrived at the bottom of a wide staircase leading to the front entrance. As directed, Wilhelmina walked at a distance, ensuring not to enter until after her stepsister was practically out of sight.

No one greeted her upon entering and, immediately, Wilhelmina searched for her friend. Aurora had either not arrived as yet or was somewhere engaged in a conversation and had not noticed Wilhelmina's arrival.

The party had not quite begun. Already, the ballroom, although spacious, was hot and airless.

The décor was breathtaking. Evenly spaced chandeliers illuminated beautiful, gleaming, tiled floors. Long tables had been set along one wall, each replete with food and punch. Punch that soon would be as unpleasantly warm as the room. Young men dressed in black with crisp white shirts and napkins over their forearms stood at the ready next to the table in case a guest required assistance of some sort. Men wearing the same uniform with coattails strolled about with trays of drinks for the newly arrived.

Depictions of handsomely dressed Jameson ancestors decorated one long solid wall. On the opposite wall, there were stained glass windows atop a series of French doors, which led to gardens and patios.

Several stations about the room had been set for guests to place glasses or appetizer plates. Lights reflected from the tall crystal vases and the ornate silver platters.

The hosts did not stand to greet guests, but mingled to give the illusion of a relaxed atmosphere. Ridiculous, of course, since every single person present wore plastered polite grins as they scanned the room for the opportunity to be one of the first to greet a Jameson.

Laverne, with Gilda in tow, made a beeline to where several prominent women huddled, sizing each other up under the guise of greetings.

Not wishing to stand aside while being ignored, Wilhelmina walked past where her stepmother and Gilda were and strolled through a set of open doors out to a patio. Although not quite the proper thing to do while alone, she always enjoyed seeing other people's gardens and the Jameson's never disappointed.

It was early yet, so only one pair of men walked about the labyrinth of bushes and trees. The garden was not as beautiful as in the spring, but it held an allure that only nature could bring this late in the year. Short trees with their golden leaves made up for flowers. Late blooming camellia added a light, sweet fragrance to the air.

Wilhelmina turned back to the ballroom just as music

from the orchestra wafted throughout the large room. Immediately, couples moved to the center to begin a familiar dance. The swaying of multicolored dresses moved in almost identical patterns as women, guided by their dance partners, glided over the pristine tile flooring. Although she had not been in the mood to attend, the music and dancing was delightful to observe.

Wilhelmina made her way to where her stepmother and Gilda conversed with a woman she didn't recognize. "This is always the grandest event," her stepmother exclaimed while she fanned her reddened face. "It is astonishingly warm for so late in the year, is it not?" she asked no one in particular and then turned to her stepdaughter. "Wilhelmina, be a dear and fetch your stepsister and me some punch."

A servant walked by with a tray of beverages and Wilhelmina reached for two glasses, passing them to the women.

Her stepmother had obviously wished to send her away by her droll expression, which Wilhelmina ignored. It was best to remain near them for the time being as she'd yet to see anyone familiar enough to speak to. Ambling about alone could turn rather boring quickly. Not that standing next to her family proved to be entertaining. At least their discomfort did provide amusement of sorts. Wilhelmina remained beside the women and watched the dancers, ensuring a pleasant curve to her lips.

After a few minutes, when she turned to get a drink for herself, the servant had disappeared. Letting out a sigh, she decided it was best to go in search of something to drink. In the meantime, she'd hopefully locate her friend.

More people entered through the front entrance, down the stairwell, and she stopped when spotting Aurora escorted by her brother and mother. Finally, she'd not have to mingle about alone or stand idly by ignored by her stepmother and stepsister.

Just as she took a step toward Aurora, a gentleman

approached her friend. Aurora's lips curved into what Wilhelmina could only describe as a forced smile and she accepted the man's escort. When he turned toward Wilhelmina, she recognized him as none other than Milford Jameson IV, the eldest son of the hosts.

This was a surprise. Wilhelmina blinked to make sure she wasn't seeing wrong. She and Aurora had just spoken earlier in the week and, although Aurora had seemed distracted, her friend had not mentioned any new acquaintance with the Jamesons.

Moving closer, Wilhelmina closed the distance to Aurora, who moved in a stilted, odd fashion. Aurora appeared almost dazed. Finally, her friend saw her and smiled warmly. "Hello, dear Willy," she said in a breathless voice and kissed her cheek. "I am so happy to see you."

Milford stood beside them, waiting politely to be acknowledged. Aurora's hand was on his arm. Once again, Aurora seemed to force a smile. "Milford, you know my dear friend, Willy, don't you?"

"Indeed, I do," he replied, giving her a curt nod. "Where are your dear mother and sister?"

Wilhelmina motioned to the far wall. "Over there. They'd love to greet you, of course."

"Perhaps after I escort this lovely creature to a dance."

Aurora's high-pitched giggle was most alarming. Wilhelmina gave her a pointed look. Why had Aurora not mentioned a possible assignation with one of the Jamesons?

Astounded at the unexpected turn of events, Wilhelmina could only look on agog as Aurora allowed Milford to lead her away.

The couple moved to the center of the dance floor. Immediately, the room was abuzz, every pair of eyes following the couple as they began to dance.

Aurora's mother had disappeared into the crowds. So when Wilhelmina spotted Aurora's cousin, Michael, beside French doors leading to a large patio, she hurried toward him to find out what brought this sudden turn of events. Something seemed wrong about the entire situation.

She and Aurora had just met for tea early in the week. She'd suspected that Aurora was troubled and questioned her. Wilhelmina had asked if something was wrong but her friend had insisted all was well. What could have possibly happened in the last two days?

"Michael?" She stepped outside to the cooler temperature. Other people mingled about, obviously also taking a breath of fresh air. The man was nowhere to be found, so she stepped down to the lower garden.

At the sound of footsteps, she whirled to find Ernest Jameson. He stood with one hand in his pocket and the other to his side. She wanted to chuckle at his pose. It was as if he purposely paused for effect. "Good evening, Mr. Jameson."

"May I escort you about the gardens, Miss Wilkins?"

"Oh," she replied, looking around in hopes of seeing Michael. Ernest Jameson had never spoken to her before and that had been more than acceptable to her. Taken aback by the request and more than a little perturbed, she attempted at a warm smile.

She didn't want to be seen with him, her stepmother and Gilda would have a fit. The topic of conversation all through dinner every day was how wonderful it would be if her stepsister caught one of the Jameson men's attention. "I appreciate the offer, but I am looking for Michael Middleton. It is imperative that I speak to him about Aurora."

"Of course," Ernest said looking around. "I don't believe I've seen him as yet."

He took her arm, his grip leaving no option but to allow him to guide her forward. "I will help you search him out. There is something I must speak to him about as well."

Instead of guiding her back to where she came from, he took her arm and turned her away. "He may have joined others over here."

She wanted to jerk her arm free of his grasp. However, afraid to offend him, she allowed him to tug her along.

When it was obvious there was no one about, Wilhelmina pulled back. "I will speak to him later. I don't hear anyone in this area."

He turned to her and leaned closer, his hand snaked about her waist. "You were searching a man out for private time in the garden. Why don't you tell me what, exactly, you had planned?" His face was much too close. The smell of whiskey on his breath made her lean way.

"What are you insinuating, Mr. Jameson? I take offense and demand you release me immediately." She attempted to pull away and when that failed, she shoved at his chest.

"Your feeble attempts to play coy are quite enchanting, Miss Wilkins." The rake pulled her against his chest.

His lips curved. Handsome as Ernest Jameson was, she felt chills when the smile didn't reach his flat eyes. "From what your sister Gilda said, you are quite friendly and welcome attention from many gentlemen. I would enjoy a turn Wilhelmina, if that is what you are after. I promise to have you back before anyone notices."

His mouth covered hers. No matter how hard she tried to push him away, he was as immobile as a stone wall. Finally she got her wits about her and lifted her leg, kneeing him between his.

With a loud "Ooof!" Ernest Jameson fell to the ground with his hands cupping his private area.

"Lout!" Wilhelmina looked down at him for an instant before whirling about and dashing away. She rushed to the house and stopped just outside the doors to ensure her hair was not in too great a state of disarray.

Just as she took a step, her arm was grabbed, bringing her around. Ernest's nostrils flared and his upper lip curled up with distaste. "Little bitch! How dare you?"

"Stop. You'll make a scene!" Wilhelmina attempted to yank her arm free, but he did not let go.

"Apologize to me," he gritted out, "or I will announce to

everyone you and I had a very private moment at your request." He leaned close and kissed her cheek. Several people turned and watched.

A woman elbowed another nearby and, before long, face after face turned to the patio.

Wilhelmina threw her head back and laughed as if he said something funny. "Oh Mr. Jameson, but no one would believe you. You are so witty." She ensured to keep her voice loud.

His smile made the blood in her veins turn to ice. "I do believe you are wrong." He turned and motioned men over. Several circled her.

Wilhelmina swallowed and looked to each one. "What are you doing?"

"Gentlemen," Ernest said to them. "I present Miss Wilhelmina Wilkins. A very friendly lady who just joined with me in the garden for a...rather enjoyable...turn. I am sure she would gladly accept a...walk about the garden with any of you, if you are so inclined."

There were loud gasps from those just inside the room as Ernest brushed past her and entered. Wilhelmina glared at the four men who'd encircled her until they moved away, but not before one of them gave a suggestive lift of his brow, his gaze moving over her.

Once again, the sounds of women gasping made her hesitate before turning to face them. Head held high, she ascended the steps and walked past the group of gossips without acknowledging them.

"Wilhelmina!" Her stepmother rushed to her, her crossed hands flat against her chest. "What is the meaning of this? Why are you outside in the gentlemen's area?"

She turned around and it was then she noticed several groups of men smoking cigars, although most ignored the goings on, a few watched with interest.

That damned Ernest had guided her to the men's balcony. She let out a breath. "I wasn't aware..."

Her stepmother dragged her further inside by the arm,

along the side of the room to where Gilda still remained. Her open-mouthed stepsister looked around the room as if hoping no one noticed the drama unfolding. Her actions only made more people look over with interest.

Wilhelmina caught sight of Aurora. Her wide eyes met Wilhelmina's before Milford leaned into her ear and whispered something that made Aurora's mouth formed an "O".

Wilhelmina pulled along by her stepmother rushed past Gilda to the front of the ballroom. When they reached the entranceway, her Lavern pointed to the doorway. "Find our coachman and go home immediately. Your reputation will be in shreds by morning. You've all but ruined Gilda's special day. I won't have you causing more damage."

"I didn't do anything...Ernest Jameson..." She stopped speaking when the hostess walked up.

"Whatever is happening?" Pearl Jameson's disapproving gaze went from Wilhelmina to her stepmother.

Instantly, her stepmother rushed to the woman. "I am not sure to be honest. My stepdaughter mistakenly walked out to the men's balcony and I believe your son was unhappy about it."

"Very much so. He told me she touched him inappropriately."

Wilhelmina couldn't believe the gall of the man. "I did no such thing. He made advances and I defended myself."

The woman gave her a disbelieving look. "Do you honestly expect me to believe that? I must ask you to leave." Her voice was raised and shrill.

The woman looked to her stepmother. "Please go, all of you."

Her stepmother gasped, her mouth opening and closing like a fish out of water. "Oh graciousness. I am so very sorry. Please..."

Pearl Jameson whirled and left.

Moments later, they rode home. The trip was very

different than just minutes earlier. Instead of glares towards her, her stepmother and stepsister yelled and berated Wilhelmina nonstop. Her father was not in attendance as he'd probably been in the library and was nowhere to be found when they were escorted out. He'd missed the entire debacle.

A sobbing Gilda sputtered accusations at Wilhelmina while her stepmother went from consoling Gilda to belittling Wilhelmina then on to join Gilda in tears.

"This is your fault," Wilhelmina told Gilda who inhaled sharply and gawked at her. "Ernest told me it was you who spread the rumor I welcomed advances from men."

"I did no such thing!" Gilda shrieked and covered her face with both hands.

"Say nothing more, Wilhelmina," her stepmother snapped. "We will deal with all of this once we get home. Your father will be most disappointed in this turn of events. Not only have you ruined your stepsister's first season, but you are also soiled. No respectable man will ever marry you now."

Once home, she was dispatched to her bedroom to remain until her father returned.


Her father's study always reminded Wilhelmina of childhood and bad news. It was there she'd been given the news of her mother's death by an ashen-faced aunt while her father grieved in another room, locked away from everyone, including her.

It was there she'd learned of the upcoming nuptials between her father and Laverne, then Tomlinson, a woman she'd never cared for.

Even now, the beautiful mahogany desk her grandfather had once owned filled her with as much sadness as the accusatory look on her father's face.

Vincent Wilkinson, was not a tall man. He was slender and handsome with silver sideburns and a thin mustache.

The man was usually a quiet, but friendly sort. Today, however, his brow was lowered as he waited for her to explain.

"Wilhelmina, what your stepmother informed me of regarding your behavior at the Jamesons' is hard for me to believe. I refused to think you could be so brazen as to be out in the gentlemen's area. And then to have touched a man inappropriately..." He stopped talking and lifted his hands as if unsure what else to say.

With her hands folded on her lap, Wilhelmina tried her best to keep from losing her composure. She'd already cried all night after returning from the party. What made her so despondent was the idea that her own father would turn against her. The last person she ever expected to believe the ridiculous accusations looked at her with disapproval and disappointment.

"I walked out to the garden in search of Michael, Aurora's cousin. Ernest Jameson came up to me and accosted me, stating he'd heard from Gilda that I welcomed advances. When he tried to pull me further into the garden, I kneed him in the groin. Then as I headed back to the stairs, I mistakenly went toward the wrong balcony. You can understand...I was distraught."

"Indeed." Her father did not sound convinced.

"Father, you must believe me. Obviously, Ernest was angry, so when he directed me up to the gentlemen's balcony..."

"Enough, Wilhelmina. It sounds like too many inconvenient happenings. Whether it is true or not, the fact Lady Jameson asked our family to leave is an embarrassment that may have caused your stepmother and stepsister to lose any invitations for the rest of Gilda's first season."

Wilhelmina tried not to roll her eyes. It always came back to the perfect, golden daughter, Gilda.

Her father leaned forward. "I'm afraid the best thing to do is to send you away until the rumors die down.

Hopefully, at least half of Gilda's season can be salvaged. I am not going to live with two hysterical women because of you acting so selfishly and reckless."

Her heart thudded against her breast. "Where will I go?"

"To Virginia, to spend the next six months with your aunt, Maureen. I believe she has need for another set of hands at her farm. You can learn to nurse while you're there."

"No!" Wilhelmina stood up. "I will not go there. Aunt Maureen detests me."

Her father continued speaking. "Once I get a response from her, you will go. I have offered to pay for your room and board, adding that you wish to learn nursing from her."

"Father..."

"Say no more. Go to your room. You will take your dinner meals there for the next few days until your stepsister and stepmother calm some."

The room swayed, but she refused to show any sign of weakness. Somehow, she'd find a way to keep from living with her dreadful aunt. The woman had never been kind, rather the opposite. As a little girl, she'd hated visiting with her mother, who'd seemed to view the visits as some sort of mission to help the woman out.

Her Aunt Maureen took glee in calling her "little pig nose". When no one looked, she pinched Wilhelmina, her nails biting deep and leaving red marks.

Wilhelmina held back the tears until inside her bedroom. The only sanctuary she'd ever known now seemed girlish and too perfect. She went to her dresser and pushed a collection of figurines aside.

Once the top of the dresser was cleared, she removed a vase of flowers from her beside table and placed its on the vanity and stacked books beside it.

She moved back and studied the dresser. It looked much better. Next, she turned to her bed. Wilhelmina removed three overstuff pillows and shoved them into her wardrobe. Once that was done, she placed an open book on the bed. Wilhelmina turned in a circle. Her eyes narrowed as she studied what else could be changed.

"No, it still looks too young. I am not a child to have all this light yellow. I don't even like yellow." She snatched a coverlet off the bed and froze. Her world was crumbling. There was nothing she could do to stop the new horrible direction of events. Surely, there was something she could do. Defeat weighed heavy, so much so that Wilhelmina crumpled to the floor with the coverlet clutched to her chest.

Lying on the floor, she cried until her entire body shook and she could barely catch her breath.

A long time later, Wilhelmina remained on the floor where she'd settled on her back to look at the ceiling. She had to do something. It was not in her nature to sit around meekly and wait for someone else to decide her future.

The next day, she'd visit Aurora. Hopefully, her friend would help her find a way to get out of the current predicament.

There was always running away, however distasteful it was. Surely, there was somewhere she could run to.

# Chapter Two

*Laurel, Montana, near Billings*

Marcus Hamilton spurred his horse forward to rush after his brother's. They raced toward the stables and, as always, it became part of the competition between them. The rascal had a good lead on him, but Marcus' horse was faster. He reached the barn just as Tobias dismounted.

When Marcus tackled Tobias from behind, both fell to the ground rolling over each other, throwing punches. The horses, smarter than their owners, moved away from the ruckus and voluntarily entered the corral area.

Tobias landed a hard punch to Marcus' jaw and he fell back, blinking away the stars that appeared. Seeing the advantage, Tobias scrambled over and sunk a fist into his brother's gut.

"Boys! Cut it out right now!" Their father's deep voice was followed by two swift kicks, one for each of them.

Tobias tumbled off of Marcus and landed on the ground next to him. Both looked up at a furious Jacob Hamilton. "Enough of this nonsense. Marcus, you have no right to be angry with your brother. It was clearly an accident that he hit you with the rope."

Marcus sat up and glared at his brother. "Twice?" When Tobias grinned, Marcus almost punched him again. But his father's presence stopped him. He rubbed at the side of his face. "I've got scratches all over the side of my face from the rope. He didn't have to be so close. Both of us know he's too good of a roper for it to be an accident."

They'd been fighting ever since Tobias found out Marcus kissed a young woman his brother had been keen on for a long time.

Ladies were scarce in the west and men often fought over the attention of what few women there were. Marcus was aware of his brother's feelings, yet had purposely set off to get Emmaline's attention. Not because he was particularly interested in her. It was more for sport as the brothers constantly competed over everything.

Tobias got up and went after the horses, not looking back at him. His brother's rounded shoulders made Marcus frown at the thought he'd hurt his brother more than intended. "Dang, Pa, you know he meant to hit me."

"And if he did? Your hot temper is going to get the best of you one of these days. Instead of being satisfied with one hit, you followed him back to brawl. I've about had enough of this rivalry between you two. If anything, you should be each other's ally."

Jacob looked his son over. "Don't go into your mother's room, either. I don't want her fretting over what happened to your face."

His father stormed away and Marcus went after his horse. Damned if his pa didn't have a way of making a man feel small using only words. He'd never understand how that was possible. Fists were what he knew. Sure, it wasn't the best way to settle a dispute, but he felt better afterwards.

Not this day, however. He should have handled today

better. Deep inside, he understood why Tobias was mad. If things were switched, he'd be pretty angry, too.

Yet, when his temper flared, he couldn't stop himself. It was as if it took over until it was out of Marcus' control.

Although the temperatures fell, instead of staying indoors after supper, Marcus sat on the front porch of the family's large cabin home and whittled a small piece of wood. Neither his brother nor father spoke to him all throughout the meal.

While his sister, Eleanor, was busy serving supper, her husband, James, kept sending him questioning looks. Marcus had just replied with a shrug.

It was best he give everyone space. Marcus was sure that while he sat outside, his father filled Eleanor and James in on what had transpired earlier.

The sun's rays cast long shadows across the fields as the wheat crops swayed with the wind. He watched as a flock of birds flew into the trees to settle for the night and let out a breath. In a few days, he'd turn thirty. He was too young to think about the rest of his years. Yet, at the same time, he was too old to not be settled with a family and children.

Billings was only a day's ride away. He considered that, perhaps, it was time he go there regularly and see about finding a wife. There were more women there, not as plentiful as back east, but surely there was someone.

The closest town, Laurel, was settled by mostly men or married couples who'd traveled west together.

He shook his head and frowned. The age milestone was affecting him in a bad way. He'd never thought about marriage and a family before. However, perhaps getting married would be a good way to stop the fighting with Tobias. Or it could be that Tobias needed to be the one to marry. Scratching his head, Marcus turned when the front door opened and his sister walked out.

Eleanor was a beauty. The eldest of the three siblings, she looked more like her mother than he or Tobias. Ever since their mother had taken to bed over an illness, Eleanor and her husband, James Ridley, had moved in to help with the household chores. Marcus admired her greatly for it.

His sister took over the housework and caring for their mother while the men worked. Her husband, a banker by trade, had given it up and worked alongside them now. James had brought their small herd of cattle and horses from their property. A sacrifice Marcus and his family appreciated.

"What are you and Tobias fighting about this time?" Eleanor gave him a disapproving look. "Please don't tell me it's about that skinny girl, Emmaline. If she has anything to do with both of you, then it's sure she's also friendly with other men from the surrounding ranches."

After a moment of silence, Marcus nodded. "I know. It's stupid. I think we're just letting off some steam. Nothin' serious." He looked to the doorway. "Mama doesn't know about the fight does she?"

"Mama asked Tobias about the split lip. He told her the rope slipped and hit him. She didn't believe it."

In spite of himself, Marcus chuckled. "Ma knows us. She can tell a mile away if we lie."

Eleanor laughed. "That's the truth. So, it's perfect timing, actually, for this news. I think we've taken care of the problem. Ma and I have done you and Tobias a huge favor."

"What did you do?" Apprehension tightened in his chest. If his sister had invited Emmaline for supper to confront them, it would not be pleasant as he was sure the woman would deny anything ever happened between them and make a big scene. How Tobias had found out was puzzling.

Chuckles sounded from indoors at whatever Tobias and his father discussed. Marcus looked over his shoulder and his brother's face transformed from smiling to a scowl. The man could hold a grudge for days.

"Come inside, Marcus, so we can tell both of you what Ma and I did." Eleanor went back inside. He waited for a few seconds, positive that whatever they plotted couldn't be good. Otherwise, why had Eleanor not said anything during supper? Not that he knew much about women, but when they put their heads together, especially two as wily as his sister and mother, there was no telling what they'd come up with.

Although reluctant to go inside, he was no coward. Marcus stood and stretched, taking his time before following his sister into the house.

He was surprised to see his mother sitting in a chair next to his father. The sight was a welcome one. Although she remained pale, her eyes were bright and she smiled up at him. "Looks like you took the worst of it this time."

"I'm sorry, Ma." Marcus went closer and placed a kiss on her cool cheek. "It's nice to see you out of bed."

"I'm having a good day. Hopefully, next week I'll be dancing," his mother said with a soft smile. She looked to Eleanor who was grinning like a loon. "Go ahead, tell the boys."

Tobias leaned forward, his gaze flitting between Eleanor and his mother. "Is something wrong?"

"Of course something is wrong," their mother admonished. "You and your brother constantly fighting. We can't have two bulls in the same pen anymore."

Marcus and Tobias looked at each other, neither wanting to be the first to look away.

"See that?" Their mother's voice broke the standoff. "It's getting to the point that one day you'll kill each other."

"I'd never kill my brother," Marcus protested. "I'm sure he wouldn't kill me."

"Don't be too sure," Tobias replied with a smirk. He sobered immediately and looked to their mother. "I'm joking, Ma. I wouldn't."

Eleanor cleared her throat. "Ma and I placed ads for the both of you in the Matrimonial Gazette back east. For mail order brides."

The room stilled as everyone went silent. Tobias and Marcus exchanged looks then each turned to stare at their sister as if to make sure they heard correctly.

A moment later, Jacob Hamilton chuckled and slapped his knee. "Well I'll be, that is a fantastic idea. The boys do need to be settled and married. That'll take care of all that energy." Their father laughed and everyone, except for Marcus and Tobias, joined in.

Tobias' round eyes pinned his sister. "What do you mean? Some woman's comin' here to marry me?"

"Once a letter arrives with one willing to, yes."

Unsure what to say, Marcus leaned back in the chair and considered the ramifications of what had just been announced. "Where are these women going to live?"

"With you," their mother answered primly. "So the both of you need to start building a house. It will be at least four months before the first bride gets here. By then, you should both be finished or close to it, anyway."

"Yes ma'am," Tobias mumbled. He stood and left toward his bedroom while Marcus remained sitting, his mind awhirl.

What exactly had just happened?

A wife? A new house? This had to be some sort of cruel joke.

# Chapter Three

Lucille, Aurora's friendly maid, opened the door when Wilhelmina arrived at the Middletons' home. It struck her as strange when she was shown to a formal sitting room and instructed to wait while the maid went to inform Aurora she'd arrived. Usually, her friend would hurry down the stairs to greet her, forgoing any formalities.

The usually talkative and bubbly Lucille gave her a worried look and hurried away before Wilhelmina could draw her into conversation.

The sitting room was elaborately decorated as Aurora's mother had a penchant for porcelain figurines and floral fabrics. Long draperies framed the tall windows overlooking the matriarch's pride and joy, her rose garden. Currently, a winter variety of blooms in pink and red barely caught Wilhelmina's attention as she paced the length of the room, anxious for her friend to appear.

Winter roses were her favorite and, on most days, she would have admired the view with more deliberation. But not this day. Today was different, everything had changed.

"Hello, Wilhelmina," Matilda Middleton stood at the entryway, in a high-collared beige dress. She held in her hand what looked to be a parasol.

The lack of warmth in the usually friendly woman brought immediate dread. "Hello, Mrs. Middleton. How are you?"

"Very well," the woman replied without smiling. "I am on my way out. Aurora should be down to see you momentarily." She swept out the door as a carriage pulled up.

"How curious," Wilhelmina whispered, looking out the window as a footman appeared and assisted Aurora's mother into the carriage. "Whatever is wrong with everyone today?" Surely, neither Mrs. Middleton nor Aurora believed the outlandish lies told by Ernest Jameson the night before.

The clock in the hallway chimed, echoing through the empty rooms. "This is ridiculous." Wilhelmina went to the doorway, intent on climbing the stairs to Aurora's room, when her friend appeared at the top of the stairs.

"Willy, I'm so sorry. I wasn't dressed." A very pale Aurora descended the stairs and greeted her with hug. "I have so much to tell you." She pulled Wilhelmina back into the sitting room just as the same maid reappeared.

"Lucille, please bring some tea," Aurora instructed, giving the maid a soft smile. "Some of your delicious short bread would be nice as well."

"Very well." Lucille bobbed her head and left.

It was evident Aurora either didn't feel well or had been crying. However, Wilhelmina didn't want to push her too much. "Are you unwell?"

After a long sigh, Aurora closed her eyes. When she opened them, they were shiny with unshed tears. "No I am not. I have to marry Milford Jameson."

"What?" Wilhelmina couldn't help raising her voice. "What do you mean you *have* to?" she asked, emphasizing the word "have". "Is he like his brother and made improper advances?"

Aurora shook her head. "No, I don't think he is as bad. He is, however, arrogant and judgmental."

"You didn't look happy to see him at the party. It seemed curious when he guided you directly to the dance floor without allowing time for you to even circulate once."

Aurora nodded. "I know. I am most unhappy about this." She squeezed Wilhelmina's hand. "What happened last night between you and Ernest?"

It was her turn to hold back tears. Wilhelmina let out a long sigh. "Your mannerisms, and even how your mother acted upon your entrance, it all struck me as strange. I needed to find out what happened. I sought to find Michael to ask about it. That is when that brute, Ernest, accosted me in the gardens."

"They accused you of improper behavior. I knew you did nothing of the sort and told them so. Of course, it did no good as Ernest remained true to course, insisting you were the one to accost him."

"Scoundrel." Wilhelmina shuddered at the turn of events in her life. "My father is sending me to Virginia. Because of this, my reputation is in shreds." A tear slipped down her cheek and she wiped it away. "Neither Stepmother nor Gilda have spoken to me since."

Aurora swallowed, her eyes shifting to the doorway as Lucille walked in with a tray. After tea was poured, she allowed for each to sip before speaking. "Mother doesn't want me to entertain you after today." She put the teacup down with so much force tea splashed over the side. "I am so sorry, Willy. I don't know what to do. Milford's mother insists that any communication with you is forbidden."

"Don't marry him, Aurora. Leave with me. Let's demand our dowry money and purchase a townhouse. We can hire maids and..."

When her friend jumped to her feet and rushed to the doorway, Wilhelmina stopped speaking. Aurora came back after assuring there was no one about. "My family is in ruins. All our money is gone. Father lost millions on a business endeavor with a railroad company. You see, the reason I'm marrying Milford is because of their money."

"Do they know your family is without financial recourse?" Wilhelmina's stomach dropped at the dire situation. "This is horrible."

23

"Yes, they know. Father is indebted to Mr. Jameson, who bailed him out of utter ruin. It was Pearl Jameson's idea that I marry Milford, as this will give their son a title being that father is an earl." Aurora's words dripped with bitterness.

Upset by her friend's plight, Wilhelmina forgot her own for the moment. "What can I do to help? There must be something. Perhaps your father to can speak to mine..."

"It's done," Aurora said, hunching her shoulders. "The engagement party invitations have been sent. Gilda is invited. I asked that they include her."

That she would not attend her childhood friend's engagement party or wedding cut Wilhelmina deeply and she grimaced at the physical pain in her chest.

"We've planned our weddings since we were little girls and now you're about to marry and I am excluded." She couldn't help the sob that escaped at knowing her childhood friend would marry a man she didn't love. Her tears were also for her own reputation, in such horrible tatters that she would never be invited to Aurora's home.

Wilhelmina could barely breathe, her chest constricting with pain and disappointment. "Perhaps it's a good thing that I am about to be sent away. The distance will help...I think."

Aurora cupped Wilhelmina's face with both hands. "This is horrible, how everything turned out for us. I don't want to be at my own wedding." When she began to cry, Wilhelmina did as well. Fate, it seemed, had dealt them both a bitter blow.

It was just days before they were both to turn nineteen years of age since they shared the same birthday.

Now they also shared another commonality.

Their futures held only bleakness.


Drained and not wanting to go home and face her stepmother and Gilda, who gloated with glee at her being sent away, Wilhelmina walked down the street. She peered into shop windows, not really seeing anything.

Her mind raced from scenario to scenario as she tried to establish what the best course of action was. How to avoid being sent to her aunt's farm in Virginia was the main focus on her mind as she walked. Anything, even servitude, was better than living with the bitter woman.

Now that it was clear she couldn't count on Aurora to leave with her, she had to decide who, if anyone, would offer some sort of idea or assistance. She needed to find help to get out of going to Virginia where she'd be hidden away in a remote ranch with no one for company but a cranky, miserly woman.

A park bench beckoned. Wilhelmina made her way to sit in the shadows of a leafless tree, its beautiful branches stretched over the bench allowing sunrays to filter through.

Once seated, she let out a breath and closed her eyes. For a moment, she'd not think of her situation. Instead, she'd enjoy the cool breeze and fresh air.

"How are you today?" A musical voice startled her. A pretty woman's sparkling green eyes met hers. Eugenia Price, a local celebrity of sorts, smiled widely. "Can I join you?"

"Yes, of course," Wilhelmina motioned to the empty seat space. "How are you Lady Price?"

Eugenia Price, American by birth, had spent her childhood in Europe and married a British Lord. They'd moved from England when both were in their twenties and taken local society by storm.

The handsome couple's parties were the place to be seen and where many an assignation both business and personal took place. The palatial home where they'd lived was both breathtaking and welcoming.

Then suddenly, Lord Price fell ill. No matter the many doctors summoned and the countless procedures performed, the forty-five year old man passed away in his prime.

Afterwards, Lady Price became a recluse. For over a year, she neither entertained, nor did she attend any gatherings. It was only during the last few months that she'd made appearances at ladies' teas and soirees.

Eugenia Price was still young and vibrant. Wilhelmina guessed her to be late thirties, perhaps. The woman let out a sigh. "I am better every day. Interesting isn't it, how those things we take for granted can disappear in a blink of an eye."

Was she speaking of her reputation? Surely, Lady Price had already heard the dreadful rumors. Wilhelmina met the woman's warm gaze. "True. I love this city. I cannot see myself living anywhere else. Yet it seems I will have to leave."

"I cannot believe how shallow our society has become. When a man is caught doing dreadful things, it's passed off with a mere shrug. But how dare a woman step out onto the wrong balcony. Suddenly, her entire life is turned upside down." She patted Wilhelmina's hand. "I am so very sorry, dear."

It was hard not to cry. Wilhelmina let out a sigh. "Thank you. You are kind."

"So what, pray tell, is your family going to do? Sending you off to a nunnery to repent?" At the woman's statement, Wilhelmina managed a smile.

"No. They are placing me with an aunt who I've not seen in years. She lives on a farm in the middle of nowhere."

Lady Price let out an exasperated huff. "Dreadful. It is that young man who should be shipped off. A couple years in the military would do him good."

"They'd just buy him a commission and have him working at a desk job with plush accommodations, I'm sure," Wilhelmina said, enjoying the woman's company.

"True," Lady Price said, nodding. She cocked her head to the side and assessed Wilhelmina. "I do have an idea. I, actually, was going to visit and inquire about you. I was hoping to get a few moments of privacy. That you are here is a happy coincidence. Perhaps, what I have to say will interest you enough to consider it." Lady Price looked to the distance, seeming to consider her next statement. "With a friend who lives out west, I've started a publication." She pulled a paper out of her handbag and unfolded it.

It was a newspaper of sorts. Across the top, in dark letters, spelled out "Matrimonial Gazette". Wilhelmina leaned forward to see a series of short snippets with pictures of different men posted.

"What is it?" Without thinking, she reached for the paper and remained transfixed, looking over the different descriptions and requests by men looking for wives. It was the most interesting thing she'd ever seen. Lady Price remained quiet as Wilhelmina turned the page and opened the newspaper to two more pages filled with different mail order bride advertisements.

"How very interesting," she finally said. She was barely able to pry her eyes from the paper to meet Eugenia Price's. "So many men."

"Exactly," Lady Price exclaimed. "This endeavor has given me a reason to get out of bed every morning. Helping these brave men who have gone west to start new lives is my cause. Each and every one of them is thoroughly investigated by my friend and her sister out west to ensure they are honorable and good-natured men before they are allowed to post an ad. As you can see, it would not be a good thing to send off a young woman only for her to meet with regrettable circumstances."

Wilhelmina, once again, scanned the pictures, her gaze going to the same one over and over. His name was Marcus Hamilton. The serious expression did not deter from his attractiveness. She wondered how a handsome man like that was not married at almost thirty.

"Why are there so many men looking for wives?" She looked to her companion. Lady Price pursed her lips.

"Men went out west to tame the territory. Most traveled in search of riches, land or adventure. Many went alone or with their family. Although there are women, those that went west mostly went with husbands. Rarely did single women go out west without good reason. So you see, Wilhelmina, there aren't enough women available."

"So your friend...how is it she lives out there? Where does she live?"

"My friend, Dahlia, more like a sister to me, and her husband, who is a banker, went west to establish a new bank. They live in Billings, Montana. She wrote me and asked if I would consider helping her in this endeavor where, for a minimal fee, men could advertise for brides."

Lady Price continued her explanation. "The young men often own land, have livestock and or earn an honest living. But they do not have a family to share their lives with."

The more she heard, the higher her interest and Wilhelmina felt it deep in her bones. Her life was about to take a sharp turn.

# Chapter Four

"She seems nice," his sister said as she peered over his shoulder at the picture. "Very pretty wouldn't you agree?"

Marcus held the letter and picture, not sure how to proceed. A part of him liked the idea of a wife. Heck, to be honest, a woman in his life made him want to grin. That he'd received a letter before Tobias was an added bonus. However, another part of him rebelled at the idea.

"Yeah. Must be something wrong." His mumbled reply was met with a glare.

"It's the second letter you've received. The first one you decided to write back to tell her you were not interested without giving Mama or me a chance to even discuss it with you. This time you won't get away with it Marcus Hamilton, I'll tell Mama."

He put the letter and photograph aside. "What about Tobias? Why don't you go pester him?"

"No letter yet. But we didn't put the ad in at the same time. We specifically requested they wait several weeks between them. First yours, then his."

That took the thrill out of the challenge. Now, he couldn't gloat to his brother he'd received a reply first.

"I'll reply to this woman...Wilhelmina and tell her I'm

interested. She won't be able to come for a while yet. By the time she gets this letter and is able to reply, it will be too cold to travel."

He'd just bought himself another two or three months.

Satisfied with his reply of accepting, Eleanor nodded. "Very well. Give me your reply when it's written. I'll post it when I go to town in the morning."

Darn it. He'd planned to put it off for at least a week or two to buy himself even more time. Marcus was hopeful that by the time the woman got his reply and explanation of how it would not be possible to travel due to weather conditions, the woman, Wilhelmina Wilkins, would change her mind.

It was still a possibility.

After his sister walked out of the room, Marcus studied the blank paper. He glanced at the scenery outside the window and considered going for a long walk.

However, Eleanor would not leave him be until the letter was written. If he put her off, she'd then worry their mother with the issue. It was best to do as asked. It was time for him to take the first step towards settling.

Not sure how to start, he considered asking Tobias, but changed his mind. Finally, after a long sigh, he began writing.


Eight weeks later, the weather had become much colder. Marcus didn't bother with a heavy coat on that particular day. With so much work to do, there was barely a need for it. The arduous activity of chopping wood kept him rather warm.

Each downfall of the ax echoed through the trees in a rhythmic percussion.

The cabin was finally completed. All that was needed now were a few finishing touches to the doorway and windows.

Thanks to help by a group of local men, the house was

built in record time. Every activity after Marcus cleared the land had miraculously gone forth without a hitch.

While his father, Tobias and James worked with the cattle and such, he'd spent the last two months building his home. Every day when he arrived at the new house, pride filled him at seeing the results of his hard work.

Furniture would have to be built and those things that he couldn't make had to be purchased. During his last trip to town, Marcus ordered a wood burning stove from the mercantile that were due to arrive any day. His sister and mother made curtains and pillows after he'd given them money to purchase fabric.

Currently, they worked on completing a quilt and pillow cover set. There was still much to be done. Strange that until having to build a home, Marcus had not considered how many items were needed to fill it.

Thankfully, his parents and Eleanor were a godsend. Somehow, his sister made the money stretch. She'd brought back from the mercantile not just the needed fabric for bedding and window dressings, but also pots, pans and other items he'd not thought about.

"You'll need a few chairs, dining table and such, still." His father rode up. "I'll help you build them if you wish."

Marcus nodded. "According to Mama, I also need to make a couple chests, a wardrobe and a cupboard for the kitchen."

His father took in the house. "You did a great job on the house, Son."

"To be honest, I'm surprised. Although I'd helped build houses before, I wasn't sure how this would go."

They walked through the front door of his new home to a large open space that would be a combination kitchen, dining and living room. Straight back from the front door were two bedrooms with an indoor privy between them.

Inside the kitchen, he'd installed a larder and another small room that could be used for storage. Overall, Marcus was proud of the house and hoped his new bride would find it acceptable.

He'd yet to add a porch, but it would be done before winter set in.

"You've got a letter." His father pulled out a crumpled envelope. "Your Ma insisted I bring it out to you. Not sure why it couldn't wait until supper."

Marcus eyed the letter not reaching for it. "Not sure I want to read it until then." Finally, he took it and shoved it into his back pocket then pushed it further down with his handkerchief. "Sometimes I wonder if Mama and Eleanor want Tobias and me to get married just so they can have women friends."

His father chuckled. "You know, come to think of it, that may be one of the reasons."

Marcus let out a breath and looked from the surroundings to his father. "What's it like, Pa? Being married."

A slow smile lifted the corners of his father's lips. "It makes you a real man fast. Sharing life with a woman is hard to explain, Son. At once, you are not just a provider, but also a protector. You are the one who is responsible for not only stability in her life, but also any children that come after. Life is never the same after marriage and, yet, it's so much better."

Marcus nodded, waiting for his father to continue.

With a hand on Marcus' shoulder, Jacob ensured he met his gaze. "Listen here. A woman can make you stronger, while at the same time so very vulnerable. All I know is that, although it's not an easy thing, I wouldn't have it any other way."

More confused than reassured, Marcus wanted his father to continue. "You knew Mama before you married her. I don't know about this." He pointed to his back pocket. "Marrying someone I never met. What if we don't get along? She could hate me at first sight."

"True," his father replied. "I've thought of that. The

best advice I can give you is to listen. You're a rash man, Marcus, act first—think later. That sort of personality will bring you more heartache than not."

It was too late to change his personality, so he resigned himself to hoping he'd manage to do better, once the bride arrived.

His father's hand dropping from his shoulder brought him out of his musing. "Don't worry, Son. Things will work themselves out. Now, how about we use some of this wood and make a couple chairs before supper?"

"What did she say?" Eleanor and his mother looked to him with more than obvious curiosity. "When is she coming?"

It was then that he realized what they were talking about. The letter was in his room, unopened. He'd looked at the envelope several times, the neat penmanship spelling out his name and the return address somewhere in Pennsylvania.

"I haven't read it yet."

"My goodness, Marcus. Why not?" Eleanor replied with a disappointed frown. "Go fetch it. You should read it at once."

"Eleanor, let the boy be," his father said, not looking up from his plate. "It's his business when he reads it and he does not have to share the contents with us. Respect your brother's privacy."

Instead of being properly chastised, his sister narrowed her eyes at Marcus. "If we don't push him, he'll just leave it unopened for days. What if she's headed here and we have no idea when to expect her or greet her in Billings?"

His mother's gaze went from Eleanor to him. "I'm sure it won't come to that. Will it, son?"

Marcus let out a slow breath. "I'll read it and make sure it doesn't." Mentally, he calculated. The days were colder, the smell of snow in the air. Soon, very soon, everything would be coated in white. Bitter temperatures would make being outdoors unbearable and most travel to the region would be put off until spring. He allowed a slow grin at his sister. "I'm sure she will not be arriving for a few months yet."

"There's still time. I am sure if she booked her travel right away, she will arrive within days."

His blood ran cold and his eyes rounded. "I haven't built a table yet. The stove hasn't arrived."

No one listened to him, they had returned to eating. He looked at Tobias who'd also turned a ghostly shade of white. His brother's brows were creased. "You think they move out here that fast?"

Marcus shrugged. "I don't know. I'll go read the letter and see what she says."


Minutes later, Marcus leaned back against his headboard and stared at the blurred lines on the paper he held. His bride was on her way. She'd thanked him for the money he'd sent for travel, insisted she was not in need of any additional funds and informed him of her estimated arrival date.

He jumped from the bed, rushed into Tobias' bedroom and verified what the current date was before returning to his room and locking the door. She would be there in a matter of days.

He mentally inventoried what had to be done at the house. Marcus followed that with thoughts of how he planned to greet her. Finally, he lost his train of thought upon realizing he'd not installed a bed yet, nor any living room chairs. There wasn't a wardrobe or cupboard, either.

The woman had to be mistaken. It was not possible that she'd arrive just as winter set in. All this time, he'd relied on the knowledge he'd not have to marry until spring, giving him at least a three-month reprieve.

Wilhelmina Wilkins informed him she would appreciate it if he arranged for them to be married immediately upon her arrival. Otherwise, she would be forced to find accommodations until they were husband and wife.

The line that took his attention most was her informing him she was traveling without a maid companion, as she did not wish to bring her "lady" with her. What type of upbringing did she come from that she had maids and such? Did she expect him to provide for a handmaiden or some sort of lady-in-waiting?

He scratched his head and let out a long breath. His sister and mother were responsible for this. Insisting he and Tobias get married.

Granted, he was a grown man and could have fought them on it. Therefore, it was not all their fault.

Two knocks on the door were followed by Eleanor's whisper. "Marcus, open the door." She knocked again and let out a loud huff. "For goodness sakes, let me in."

It was useless to not let the nosy woman in, so he stood and opened the door. She rushed to his bed and looked down at the letter. "What does she say?" Her eyes were bright, lips parted with anticipation of whatever he would say.

"She'll be here in a few days. I am not ready, we don't have a stove or a bed..." he paused and cleared his throat. "She's probably already traveling here."

Eleanor laughed and clutched her hands together. "How positively exciting! I can't wait to meet her."

When she noticed he frowned, her eyebrows rose. "Please don't tell me you are scared."

"I am not scared. What I am is not ready. I don't know why I let you and Mama talk me into this."

Her smile returned. "You'll thank us as soon as you are settled into your new life." She glanced at the letter again. "What else did she say?"

"Something about not traveling with a companion or a maid."

At this, Eleanor scowled. "Maid?"

"That's what she wrote."

"Oh goodness. I wonder if she is some sort of high born. It could be hard for her to adjust to our style of life."

He blew out a long breath. "And that, Sister, is why this entire idea is probably a mistake. I can't give her anything close to a pampered life."

Refusing to lose her positive outlook, Eleanor smiled widely. "I think she will be perfect. She's pretty by the picture she sent and, according to her introduction letter, wishes to start a new life."


That night, the bright full moon shined through the window across his bed. Marcus remained awake, listening to nature's nocturnal symphony as he went over everything that he had to do to prepare for his wife's arrival.

A wife. Very soon, he'd have a winter bride.

# Chapter Five

The train chugged along at a fast pace, the cars jostling side to side. The movement lulled its passengers into a fitful slumber as mile after mile was traversed.

No matter how Wilhelmina shifted, it was virtually impossible to get comfortable on the hard bench. One more day, just another long day, and she'd arrive at her destination. From Laurel, she'd be traveling by either coach or... Wilhelmina frowned. How would she be traveling to her new home? Did people out in the west own coaches?

From what she'd been informed by Lady Price, the way of life in the west was very different than the city. She'd have to learn to preplan things she took for granted, like shopping for essentials. Often times, trips to purchase necessities meant traveling long distances to reach the local mercantile and such.

Additionally, many households did not hire household help. Or if they did, the workers were local, indigenous people who may or may not speak English.

She peered out to the passing landscape, but it was much too dark to see more than the blurred outlines of whatever they passed. The cabin of the train was rank, stale and in much need of fresh air to clear out the lingering smell of unwashed bodies and packed food past its prime.

A man snored somewhere in the space. His loud exhalations mixed with the sounds of other, softer sleep noise.

Wilhelmina jerked awake when her head fell forward and she rearranged a folded blanket to make a pillow. Once morning arrived, it would be time to worry about all that she faced. For now, she was in dire need of sleep.

As her eyes closed, a picture of a tall, handsome man formed. His hand reached up, assisting her down from the train. Once Wilhelmina touched the ground, he gallantly bowed in welcome.

Upon the formal greeting, he took her hand and pressed a soft kiss to her knuckles. He assured her he would be a gentleman and allow her time to get to know him before they became intimate.

His kind eyes were warm as he placed her hand into the nook of his arm and guided her away from the noise and ruckus of the crowds at the platform. Then ensuring she was properly ensconced in a plush coach, he climbed in beside her and instructed the coachman to carry them away to their romantic destination.

Wilhelmina's lips curved as a yawn escaped and then sleep claimed her.


"Laurel Station!" a conductor called out for the tenth time it seemed. The train slowed to a crawl as the passengers scrambled to put all their belongings together. The windows were lowered, allowing in cold fresh air. Wilhelmina sat primly in her seat. At her feet, sat the trunk filled with her belongings and her oversized carpetbag rested atop that. Her other things were being mailed to her by Lady Price. They would arrive in another week or so.

The landscape outside was not much different than it had been for the last day. Instead of buildings and roads, there were long expanses of rolling hills and meadows flanked by tall mountains.

Wilhelmina couldn't get over the difference between Montana and where she came from. Although she spotted buildings in the distance, this was nothing like Philadelphia.

There were fields with small groupings of trees in the wide expanses of land. The scene was dotted with cattle grazing. People traveled by horseback and open wagons more than coaches.

She wondered how women traveled when alone. Were there coaches for hire? It had not occurred to her to ask so many things when writing Marcus Hamilton. Now, it was through experience that she would learn the answers, it seemed.

A crying child ran past where she sat as a woman chased close behind. "Jimmy, stop this instant! You're going to fall." The harried woman gave her an apologetic look before finally grabbing the boy's arm. The kid was red faced at this point, mouth wide open as he shrieked in protest.

While the woman attempted to comfort the toddler, Wilhelmina could only watch and relate to the boy. It would be wonderful to get away from the chaos and noise of the passengers attempting to gather their belongings and wits after so many days on a cramped, just as noisy train.

Wilhelmina's lips curved at remembering what awaited her. A man who would court and romance her, knowing they would share a lifetime together. Her husband-to-be was handsome and, by his letters and penmanship, a complete gentleman. Although his letters had been brief and to the point, she was able to glean from reading between the lines a deeper message of courtship and restraint.

Finally, the train heaved to a slow stop. The resonances of screeching along with reverberations and jolts were a most glorious occurrence, indeed. Excited passengers on the platform side lowered windows and looked out, some already waving and calling out at recognizing those waiting for them.

Wilhelmina searched the sea of people on the platform to see if any looked familiar. Several men were gathered along the wall of the station and she slowly scanned every face until giving up. It was pointless. With so much commotion, she could not get a clear look. The doors opened and people began moving while lugging or dragging their possessions.

Her trunk was much too large for her to carry alone. Wilhelmina peered out and noticed that young men rushed to and fro helping passengers disembark. Some carried suitcases and such to the platform, placing them in neat piles and standing by them until paid.

Once again, she looked to the line of men along the wall. They'd diminished in number as some had moved forward to greet someone disembarking or worked on some sort of railroad job. Of those that remained, none looked like the man in the photograph. Letting out a huff, she stood and moved to the doorway. Upon catching a young man's attention, she waved him over. "I require assistance with a large trunk, please."

Finally, a long while later, Wilhelmina found herself settled onto a bench with her possessions neatly placed beside it. She stood once again and searched the platform for someone who seemed to be looking for her. Other than a few meandering people and passengers waiting for transport, the crowd had shrunk to only a few stragglers.

"Sir, where can I get something to eat?" she asked an older man who was sweeping the platform. "And can I pay someone to watch my things?"

The older man's face creased when he smiled widely. "I am Bert Simpson. I work here at the station. I can get your things put away in the box office where no one will bother them." He whistled and motioned for a young man. "Billy, git over here and move the lady's things into my office."

Bert turned back to her. "If you like, the local dining establishment is just over there. Just walk on this side of the street, ma'am. There is a saloon on the other side and you don't want to walk in front of it. Always some commotion in there."

"Oh goodness. I'd not considered that." Wilhelmina looked to where the man motioned. "Mr. Simpson, do you know Marcus Hamilton? He was supposed to meet me here."

"Marcus? I know that young man and his family. Fine people, those Hamiltons. They own land about a couple hours away. Jacob Hamilton, Marcus' father, is a personal friend." The man scratched his head. "I thought to have seen Marcus earlier when he rode past towards town just before your train arrived. He's here in town."

"Thank you." Wilhelmina lifted her skirts. What could have kept the man from coming back upon hearing the train arrive? She was not happy at the fact that he left her alone to fend for herself. Although not a huge town, Laurel was much too unfamiliar of a place for her to find him. She'd go to the eating establishment and get a meal. After that, she'd inquire about a room and send a note to the Hamiltons announcing her arrival. Perhaps, the letter she'd sent had not arrived. Now that would be troublesome.

It was a short walk to the main street and she watched with interest as people bustled to and fro. Riders on horseback rushed past as did several wagons either laden with items or people. It was curious not to see many carriages. Instead, families seemed to travel by wagon, sitting precariously on a bench next to whoever handled the reins.

Her skirts dragged on the dirty road and she tried her best to lift them to keep from catching on nails or the wooden planks of the walkway. Finally, she caught sight of the eatery.

Just then, a commotion broke out across the street.

Men yelled and several people rushed from the front of the saloon as a pair of men crashed out through the front doors. A whirlwind of punches and growls, the two rolled around into the middle of the road, oblivious to passersby. A wagon veered around them, barely slowing as one of the men lifted the other by the shirt collar and hit him so hard that the hapless victim flew a few feet, landing with a loud humph.

Wilhelmina stood with her back against the wall, unable to look away from the spectacle. She'd never witnessed such a brutal display of animosity. Just then, the man who'd been punched got up and rushed the taller one and both began to hit one another with renewed vigor.

A third man rushed over, pulled a gun and shot into the air. Wilhelmina and several other women screamed at the loud sound.

It startled the brawlers to stop. Both men lay on their backs, their chests heaving. It was then Wilhelmina noticed the man who'd shot wore a tin star pinned to his chest. A sheriff had come and would surely drag the troublemakers away to jail. A much-deserved spell behind bars would serve them right.

Wilhelmina was finally able to lower her hands from her chest where she'd clutched her small reticule as if it would protect her. With wide eyes, she watched as the sheriff scolded the men who looked to be properly chastised, their eyes downcast and boots scratching at the ground.

"Brutes." A young woman came to stand next to Wilhelmina. "I don't know why these men don't expend all their energy doing something useful." She shook her head, blonde, tight curls bouncing, and smiled at Wilhelmina. "You must be new in town by the pale, frightened look on your face."

"Yes, I just arrived. I'm Wilhelmina Wilkins." She held out her hand.

The blonde took her hand. "Isabel Ward. My father is the preacher here in Laurel. There he is now."

They watched as a clergyman neared and took one of the fighters by the arm and pulled him towards where she and Isabel stood.

Isabel laughed. "Looks like Marcus is in big trouble now."

Just then, the tall man who allowed the preacher to guide him toward her looked up. His bright hazel eyes met hers. Wilhelmina lost her breath and looked to her new acquaintance. "What did you say?"

"I said that Marcus Hamilton is in trouble. He's such a hothead. Like a bull in a pen."

Wilhelmina looked to the man again. Her soon to be husband had a trickle of blood trailing from the corner of his mouth. The cut expanded when he grinned at her.

Lord help her.

# Chapter Six

Marcus wasn't sure why he grinned other than the preacher's words made him want to laugh. That he'd forgotten all about his troubles for a few minutes while brawling helped clear his head.

The grin left when his lip ached and upon meeting the gaze of disapproval of the most beautiful woman he'd ever laid eyes on.

Annoyed at the thought he'd never be able to get to know her, he was instantly reminded that his soon to be wife could have been on the train that arrived moments earlier.

"Pastor Ward, I do apologize for my behavior and understand you wish to speak to me about it. However, I have to go to the station and see if my bride arrived." He'd already met with the man about marrying him as soon as Wilhelmina Wilkins arrived. As much as he didn't want to marry a total stranger at first sight, it would not be a good idea to take her home without being married.

"Have you considered the picture you will present upon meeting her? Your right eye will swell shut and your mouth is cut open." Pastor Ward didn't raise his voice while speaking, yet every word seemed loud and clear. The clergyman released his arm. "Mind your manners, there's my daughter and another lady."

The fact the pastor felt such a warning was needed annoyed him. But under the circumstances, he couldn't blame him. "Yes sir."

The woman who stood next to the pastor's daughter had turned some sort of green shade. Her eyes widened more and more as he and the pastor walked closer. Maybe his face was a fright. He looked down and wiped at his mouth with his torn sleeve. "I should probably go wash my face."

"Hello, Father," Isabel Ward said, looking from her father to him. "Marcus." It was evident she was not impressed by what she'd seen.

There was a beat of silence before Pastor Ward looked to the pretty woman who'd yet to look away. Her study of him made Marcus want to shuffle his feet. "I am George Ward, Isabel's father." He motioned to Marcus. "And believe it or not, this man is not as he presents himself. Marcus Hamilton."

If possible, the woman paled further. "N-nice to meet you...I am Wilhelmina Wilkins."

The ground shifted and Marcus reached out with both arms to steady himself on the nearby porch post. He first searched the pastor's face and then looked to Isabel who frowned back.

Isabel crossed her arms and peered at him with both eyebrows lifted. "Whatever is wrong with you, Marcus? Fist fighting in the middle of town in bright daylight. Your mother will hear about this and she will be most displeased."

He finally met Wilhelmina's gaze. The woman was dressed in finery from the top of her head, where a small hat was perched, to her fitted jacket over an obviously expensive gown.

Clutched in her hands was a small bag of sorts that matched her dress. She squeezed it tighter upon his inspection.

The pastor looked from him to Wilhelmina. "Don't tell me this is the woman you are here to meet?" He seemed to find humor in the situation as his eyes twinkled with barely hidden mirth. "Well, I'll be."

"What?" It was Isabel's turn to stare, her eyes and mouth wide. "Oh no."

Finally, Wilhelmina blinked and let out a soft breath. "Mr. Hamilton, I expected to be greeted at the train station."

He swallowed and looked to the pastor who didn't offer any help. "I apologize...I was..."

"Otherwise detained?" She lifted a perfectly formed eyebrow and glanced toward the saloon. "I am not sure we are suited at all. I will make arrangements to return home at once." She turned to the other two people and gave them a polite smile. "Can you instruct me as to where I can find accommodations for a few days?"

Pastor Ward nudged Marcus.

"I will escort you to a meal and make arrangements for your belongings to be picked up." Marcus motioned toward a small eatery. "If you would give me a moment, I need to wash up before I will be fit to be seen with you."

"Why don't we have tea while we wait?" Isabel thankfully added. "I'm sure this will all work itself out." She shook her head and gave Marcus a pointed look. "You will learn life is much different here. And although Marcus has not made the best of impressions, he has some redeeming qualities."

The pastor's daughter, once again, looked to Marcus. "Join us after you clean up."

Being Isabel had never been friendly to him, but preferred Eleanor's company, he was intrigued to hear what those particular redeeming qualities were. His intended looked at him for a moment then offered a reluctant nod to Isabel.

"Very well. Although at the moment, I am not so sure any quality could redeem what I just witnessed."

46

As Wilhelmina and Isabel walked away, both turned to look at him. Neither expression made him feel good about the situation.

Pastor Ward remained next to him. "I'd also suggest you find a clean shirt and perhaps some very cold item to press against that eye." The pastor tapped his shoulder. "Not a good first impression, Marcus."

Whistling, he followed after the women.

Truer words had never been spoken. What had he been thinking, going to the saloon to wait for the train? Instead, he could have used the time more wisely and purchased some needed things at the mercantile. He blamed the situation on his being on edge, unsure of what would happen once his bride-to-be arrived.

Marcus hurried to a friend's home to fetch a shirt and wash up.

Evan Jones looked up from where he sat reading. "Needing a few stitches today?" Evan's gaze traveled across Marcus' face to his bloody knuckles. "I heard the commotion outside and a pair of woman came to take refuge in here." He smiled and shook his head, moving closer. "The lip can go without stitching. Your eye will probably be all right in a couple days."

"I need to borrow a shirt and wash up," Marcus said, already moving to the man's living quarters. "I have a...visitor."

Evan followed him. "Is that so? Who is visiting you?"

"No one you know." He went to a trunk, opened it and pulled out a shirt. "This will do." After yanking his torn and dirty one off, he went to a basin and poured water into it.

"Help yourself," Evan said, leaning on the doorjamb, his arms crossed. "Who's the woman?"

He lowered his face and splashed water onto it.

Immediately, a picture of the beautiful woman with Pastor Ward and his daughter came to mind. "Ma and Eleanor wrote off for a mail order bride. She came on the train today."

His friend's chuckle irritated him. "Did she see the fight?"

Marcus nodded. "And wants to go back home." Instead of feeling relief at the thought of Wilhelmina leaving, disappointment nudged. "She can't leave, of course."

"Why not?"

"Because I won't allow it."

This time, Evan laughed. "This, I have got to see. Where is your not to be bride?"

"At the restaurant down the street with Pastor Ward and his daughter."

"I'll go with you."

Marcus sized up his friend. At thirty-two, Evan Jones was in his prime. With dark blond hair and bright brown eyes behind spectacles, he could have been plain of face. But no, Evan was tall, wide shouldered and attractive. A doctor, he also had education and a viable, stable income.

"No you won't."

"Afraid of competition?" Evan guessed exactly what Marcus feared. After the horrible first impression, a circus chimp would prove a better match for the fair Wilhelmina.

"I would rather not have more of an audience than I will already with the preacher and his daughter there." Marcus shoved Evan's shirt into this pants. "I'll bring your shirt back after it's washed. Thank you."

"Not a problem, apparently," Evan replied with a frown. "I like that shirt, so don't tear it up."

The doctor went to another room and returned with gauze. The smell of antiseptic made Marcus cringe even before the stinging liquid was pressed to his lip.

"Ouch," he groaned. He attempted to remain still when Evan rubbed at another nick on his jaw.

"There's not much I can do about the eye. Best to press a wet cloth against it a bit before leaving."

Marcus was feeling a bit more prepared to meet the woman who would hopefully be his wife. It struck him as odd that immediately upon meeting her, ownership settled within. He hesitated in front of Evan's house. He thought back and considered all this was a waste of time and she'd continue to insist on leaving.

What would he feel if she insisted on returning home?

Marcus smoothed the shirt and lowered his shoulders. He'd better make a better impression over the meal if he hoped to change her mind.

The sky was clear, a bright blue. In spite of the frigid air, the sun felt warm on his back. It was still early, just past noon.

The time of day gave him a few hours to convince Wilhelmina to marry him so they could head home and be there before too late.

If she refused, they'd both remain the night and that meant she would have the option of the next train out of Laurel. The train would arrive the day after.


In spite of the dread at seeing her intended again, Wilhelmina found herself enjoying Isabel Ward's company. From what the young woman told her, life in the west was much more different than she'd expected. Everything from modes of transportation, ways of dressing and the temperament of the local society, as it was, were nothing like back home.

From what she observed around her, the women dressed with less regalia. The men often wore thick, wool overcoats. Although most of the men donned hats, many of the coverings looked well worn, the same for shoes. She'd noticed Isabel's shoes were more serviceable than fashionable. Her overcoat was worn to protect from the cold air and not as a fashion statement.

Wilhelmina had thought herself prepared with a fitted jacket and cape, but the cold air had managed to seep through the clothing. She'd been shivering by the time she and her companions arrived at the eatery.

The preacher made his excuses after finishing his coffee and informed them he'd return for Isabel within the hour. He asked that Wilhelmina take time to listen to Marcus and speak to him for a bit before making the rash decision to return home.

Once her father left, Isabel gave Wilhelmina a soft smile. "I certainly understand your trepidation after seeing the ruckus from the saloon. But you must understand, most men here are untamed. Although their mothers try their best, there simply aren't enough women to force them to be more polite in public." Isabel let out a sigh. "Some are better disposed than others. Marcus is normally easygoing, although he does have a quick temper. He will fight first and then, afterwards, usually remains friends with whoever he traded punches with."

"Do you have a brother?" Wilhelmina asked, unable to keep from smiling. "Is he as untamed?"

"Oh yes," Isabel replied rapidly. "Jonas and father constantly argue over my brother's refusal to mature. Although not as hot tempered as Marcus, he is forever trying his luck at different ventures that cost him dearly."

Wilhelmina wondered at the way of life in the west. Certainly, there were trades the men could do. And obviously, more and more people, especially women, came west. "I think they are clinging to the notion of the untamed west to keep from minding their manners. In my opinion, there is never an excuse for such foolish behavior."

"You are correct, Miss Wilkins." Marcus Hamilton stood beside her, his bright hazel eyes taking her in. Upon closer inspection, his bruising was not as bad as she'd first thought. Although his right eye was swollen, it was still open. "I apologize for my behavior and for not greeting you at the train station today." He hesitated and looked to her companion. "Miss Ward, how are you today?"

He remained standing, for which Wilhelmina was grateful. At least he wasn't totally without some kind of decorum.

When she didn't speak, Isabel motioned to the chair her father had just vacated. "Please join us, Marcus."

He pulled the chair back. Wood scratched across the floor, the sound vibrating up her spine. Finally, Marcus lowered his large frame onto the chair directly across from her and she couldn't help but look directly at him.

At seeing the handsome man so close, her breath caught. Apparently, she'd been so caught off guard by the fistfight and subsequent shock that she'd not noticed how attractive Marcus Hamilton was. Even with a swollen eye and cut lip, he was more than any woman could hope for in a husband. Tall and broad shouldered, he fit comfortably into the role of rancher and cowboy.

She wondered how he would react to knowing her plans remained firm. No matter how good looking or handsome a man was, Wilhelmina could not see spending the rest of her life with a ruffian.

"Mr. Hamilton, I must tell you I'm appalled by your behavior. Not only did you not greet me, but also you left me to fend for my personal belongings and find my way into town. I won't even discuss your other actions."

Upon letting out a huff, she lifted her chin to look down her nose at him, failing only because he was so much taller even when seated.

His brows came together and he rolled his head, stretching out his neck. To all outward appearances, he was more bored than contrite. But she'd seen the slight widening of his eyes while she spoke and the fact her words affected him, for some reason, made her feel better.

"I apologize profusely. I understand why my behavior gives you a bad impression. However, I assure you, it is not an indication of how your life here will be." He raked his fingers through his wavy hair and looked up just as a woman came and refilled their tea. He asked for water and nothing else then gulped down the entire contents before the woman left, so she refilled it.

In truth, Wilhelmina began to doubt her decision to return east. Her prospects were to live alone in Philadelphia, shunned by society for doing so, or moving to live with her aunt. The latter made her shudder.

"If I were to stay, Mr. Hamilton, I would like a reprieve on the marriage. I need time to ensure this is not a huge mistake."

"No." He leaned forward, placing his elbow on the table. "We get married today or not at all. You accepted my proposal, Miss Wilkins. We have an agreement. I will be a good husband and I will never give you cause to regret your decision to marry me. You will be treated well and respected. The one thing I ask is that you and I marry today."

At a loss for words, she looked to Isabel.

Instead of being shocked, Isabel smiled, looking from one to the other. "How romantic," she exclaimed and rested her chin on her palm, waiting for whatever happened next.

"I do not agree, Isabel. This is must objectionable."

Both Marcus and Isabel frowned, obviously not sure what she meant. Wilhelmina lifted her cup and sipped, looking into Marcus' eyes over the rim of the cup. "I am not sure how to reply."

"No need. We'll go to Pastor Ward's house, get married and, after picking up your belongings, we will go home."

Her face heated and she was sure it reddened, a combination of confusion and anger. On one hand, the fact he was taking charge in such a frank and open manner was quite attractive. On the other, how dare the man order her about? "You are not going to tell me what I must do. I make my own decisions." She sat erect and scanned the interior of the restaurant. The people at the neighboring tables all watched, enthralled.

To make matters worse, the two other women in the room looked at Marcus as if he were the most admirable of men. The man had just rolled around in the middle of the street for goodness sakes. People in polite society would be shunning him.

Yet, why was she still sitting there considering his proposition and having a hard time?

If she were to be totally frank with herself, why the women in the room admired the man was, indeed, understandable. A handsome, rugged man who took charge was the flesh and bone hero of every romance novel.

"Very well, Mr. Hamilton. Let us go."

His mouth fell open and he looked to Isabel as if to confirm her words. The young woman stood with Wilhelmina and grinned at him. "Pay the tab and come along, Marcus. Wilhelmina and I will await you at my home."

"Don't forget to pick up my luggage," Wilhelmina added in a flat tone. "Please try not to get into a fight along the way."

# Chapter Seven

The pastor's house was on a corner at the edge of town. It was built next to a small, but quite beautiful chapel.

Exhaustion began to set in just as Wilhelmina sunk into a small, overstuffed chair. It was early afternoon on her first day in Montana and already so much had occurred.

Her mind was awhirl at considering the situation. If things were different, she'd give Marcus Hamilton a piece of her mind and continue forth without considering the man for marriage. He'd have to prove himself to her, by courtship and interaction over a period of time.

So far from home and without the option of returning, this was her first test. The idea of a return train ride made her want to weep.

Not seeming at all discomfited, Isabel went about adding a log to the fire in the hearth. She was humming as she sat in another chair. "I love your dress. Women here always look forward to seeing what new arrivals wear. I am sure everyone will be coming around to see you whenever you and Marcus come to town, just to see what you wear."

The young woman continued chatting and asking Wilhelmina questions about fashion and such. The distraction from her situation helped settle her some.

Wilhelmina yawned and covered her mouth. "I'm so sorry. It's been an exhausting few days."

Isabel nodded in understanding. "I understand. Train travel is not easy, especially for so long a distance."

More than anything, at the moment, to lie upon a comfortable bed and sleep for hours would be a wish come true. Instead, there was a knock at the door announcing her husband-to-be had arrived. When the front door opened and Marcus Hamilton stepped inside, her heart tumbled and something akin to butterflies fluttered in her stomach.

A most disturbing reaction for sure as she'd barely met the man. True, he was for all intents and purposes, her fiancé, but that could change at any moment.

Pastor Ward walked into the room and greeted Marcus with a familiarity that spoke well of their relationship. The clergyman asked him to sit and he did so, on the chair next to hers. The pastor then sat opposite them and placed his hands on his knees looking from one to the other.

"I have considered the situation. Knowing Marcus the way I do, I recommend you go through with the marriage, Miss Wilkins. You will not want for a better, more honorable husband. And although he is of a quick temper, he has never raised his voice or his hand to any woman."

Wilhelmina remained speechless, looking at the pastor who reached for his bible. How to rebut such a statement? Of course, it was what she wished more than anything, to be married to an honorable man who would treat her well. Her main objections at the moment were his abhorrent behavior just hours earlier and lack of manners at not meeting her upon arrival. But Pastor Ward's words had done quite a bit to set her mind at ease.

Marcus looked to her, his gold-speckled eyes warm when meeting hers. "I do wish to marry you, Miss Wilkins. As Pastor Ward claims, I will strive to be a good husband."

"However," the pastor said as he held up a hand. "I feel you should wait at a few days and allow for courtship. Miss Wilkes will remain here in our home for at least a week."

Marcus' eyes rounded. "That's a long time. The weather may not hold up."

"It's not long enough," the pastor interrupted. "Besides, she's exhausted. It's much too soon to take her to your home."

Marcus grumbled under his breath then nodded. "Of course." Everyone looked to Wilhelmina who could barely put a thought together.

She was much too tired to form any kind of argument. Truth be told, she'd marry a mule at this point if it meant being left alone to rest.

"I am so tired. At this point, I can only say the pastor makes the most sense. I came this far under the agreement to marry you," she said, looking to Marcus. "I will keep my word, but would like a few days reprieve, please."

"Marcus," the pastor said. "Why don't you come back later this evening after Miss Wilkins rests and visit with her? Then return in two days. At that time, after you spend some time together, she can give a final decision."

The pastor walked out of the room with Isabel in tow to give them privacy. Wilhelmina swallowed, unsure of what to say to the man who frowned while staring at the fire.

"I suppose you're angry."

His wide shoulders lifted and lowered. "No, just disappointed." He looked to her with a curve to his lips. "My sister and Ma will be even more so. They're looking forward to meeting you." His brows came together and he huffed. "Both will give me a piece of their minds once they find out what happened."

It was her turn to smile. "I suppose they will."

He stood and held his hat in his left hand. "I look forward to our evening visit. Rest well, Miss Wilkins."

Much to Wilhelmina's dismay, the afternoon had turned to evening when she woke. Voices from the front room and the smell of food pulled her from her slumber. In a hurry, she dashed from the bed and splashed water on her face from the basin thoughtfully filled by Isabel or a maid, she wasn't sure. Afterward, she brushed her hair and pinned it away from her face. Once she felt presentable enough for company, it was time to face her fiancé for a second time.

Upon entering the dining room, everyone looked up. Isabel reacted first by motioning to a chair. The men stood as she neared and Wilhelmina sat without making eye contact.

"How did you rest, Wilhelmina?" Pastor Ward asked, his kind eyes meeting hers. "I assume it wasn't long enough of a nap."

"Very comfortably, thank you."

When she looked to Marcus, his darkened gaze met hers and much to her mortification, a heated flush rose to her cheeks.

Isabel, who seemed not to run out of topics of discussion, helped maintain a comfortable flow of conversation while they ate. The food was delicious. There was a generous portion of mashed potatoes with meat and gravy along with freshly baked bread.

Once they finished eating, Wilhelmina offered to assist the maid and Isabel with clean up. She was hurried out of the room and told to spend time with Marcus.

"Would you care to walk outside, Miss Wilkins?"

Although she wasn't anxious to be exposed to the cold, Wilhelmina wanted some private time to speak with Marcus. "Very well. I will retrieve my cloak."

"You will require something warmer than what you wore earlier. I stopped by the mercantile and purchased a more suitable coat. You can order one more to your liking later if you wish."

On a peg hung a beautiful, thick, dark brown coat. Wilhelmina reached for it, her fingers sinking into the dense fur lining. "Thank you. I love it."

He assisted her into the coat and, within seconds, warmth engulfed her. They walked out to find the sun had begun to set. Wilhelmina allowed him to take her elbow and assist her down the front porch steps onto the boardwalk.

"I will give you a tour of our town. Although there is little to see right now, more is planned." Marcus described each building and who either lived in the space or was the proprietor of the business. She found it interesting how many people lived above their business and not in a separate house.

Most had closed for the day. The only places remaining open were the hotel and the saloon, which he made sure to walk past on the opposite side of the street.

There were few people out and about, but those who were immediately came to them to be introduced to Wilhelmina. Each person gave a glowing recommendation of her soon to be husband until she began to wonder if, perhaps, they were honest or just hoped marriage would settle him down.

Marcus motioned to a small building with a bell set up in front. "That is our school house. Our current teacher is one of the farmers' wives, so class is only held twice a week. A new schoolmarm was expected to arrive last month. From what I understand, she's been detained by some sort of family illness."

Wilhelmina studied him for a moment. Marcus' one eye was swollen almost shut now and he sported purple bruising around his mouth and jaw. He would not make the most appropriate groom, but Wilhelmina's mind was made up. If she came this far and made a commitment to do something, then she'd follow through. The hot-tempered man would just have to deal with the consequences.

"Why did you post an ad for a wife? It seems to me, you are well liked and, although there aren't many women here, I'm sure you would not have a problem in finding a wife."

His gaze moved to the side as he considered how to reply. "I didn't place the ad. My mother decided it was the best way to get my brother and me settled."

"Oh." A troublesome thought occurred. "So you are forced into this?"

"Not at all," he replied readjusting his hat. "As a matter of fact, I planned to get married. I just wasn't sure how I'd go about finding a wife." He grinned then grimaced as it probably smarted with his split lip.

"Sorry about my appearance. I know it's not attractive and probably a bit frightening."

She nodded. "A bit...yes. Marcus?"

"Yes, Miss Wilkins?"

"What if we are not suited? What would you do if, after all this, you realize we've made a huge mistake?" The question she posed to him was the same she'd been repeating to herself since agreeing to the marriage.

"We will make vow to each other. I am of a thought that those promises will be what should keep us together. If and when we have any problems, we can remind each other of that." His hazel eyes roamed over her face and his brows lowered. "I do believe physical attraction is a good start. I find you beautiful, Miss Wilkins."

Wilhelmina could not help her eyes from rounding. Unlike any man in her past who may have declared to find her attractive, Marcus' words sunk in and made her very glad to hear them. At the same time, it was quite unsettling when heat rushed to her cheeks.

"Thank you. Please call me Wilhelmina. We are to be married after all."

His lips curved. "Very well, Wilhelmina. I should escort you back. It's much too cold to keep you out here for so long."

Upon arriving at the front porch, Marcus lifted her hand and pressed a kiss to the back of it. "I will remain here in

59

town and come see about you tomorrow. Is late morning a good time?"

Flustered at his closeness and not quite sure what, if anything, the Ward's had planned, she nodded. "I think so, yes."

Upon the door being opened by a bright-eyed Isabel, Marcus tipped his hat and took his leave.

Isabel tugged at her right hand. "Hurry inside. It's freezing out there. Come in and sit by the fire."

They settled into chairs where Isabel already had a pot of tea sitting next to the fire. "I figured you'd want something warm to drink."

Wilhelmina looked to the door. "Where do you think Marcus will spend the night?"

"Probably at Dr. Jones' house. They are good friends. Marcus and his brother, Tobias, often sleep there when they come into town."

She wondered about her intended's family, but was too tired to ask. Once she sipped the tea, she wanted to go to bed.

Isabel poured the tea and handed her the first cup. "Did he kiss you? Where did you go?" Although her new friend was overly curious, Wilhelmina liked Isabel.

"No he did not kiss me, other than my hand. We walked down the boardwalk to the school house and back."

"Oh," Isabel said downturned lips.

Morning came too soon but Wilhelmina felt remarkably rested after deciding she'd not put off Marcus. It was best to proceed as planned and marry. Since there wasn't really a good reason other than her nerves to put it off, she preferred to move forward and start her new life.

Determination would be best in this instance and for the months to come. There was much to learn and become accustomed to. Although she'd considered herself prepared for the roughness of the west, the truth was, it turned out to be much more underdeveloped than she ever expected. It would take some time to get used to the fact everything there was rudimentary. Not in a bad way, but obvious things from buildings to clothing was fashioned to withstand the elements and not to impress.

Over breakfast, the pastor and Isabel ate with gusto, both peppering her with questions about life in Philadelphia. She imagined one day she'd act the same when meeting someone who came from out east.

"Have you made a decision, young lady, regarding Marcus? Will you marry him in a few days?" The pastor's warm gaze rested on her for a moment. "Whatever your decision is, know that my daughter and I will support you."

Wilhelmina put her fork down and sighed. "I have. I will marry him and I would rather do it today, if possible. I don't want to impose on your hospitality. Not only that, but I came with the expectation of marrying right away and beginning a new life with him."

"That's good news," Isabel exclaimed, bouncing in her seat and clapping. "I'll help fix your hair."

The pastor smiled at his daughter. "I will inform Marcus when he arrives. Once you're finished with breakfast, it's best you get ready. I know these things take time. However, young lady, you do not put us out in any way. Quite the contrary. Isabel loves to have company."

Isabel bobbed her head while grinning. "It was so very nice to have you here."

When they finished eating, Isabel and Wilhelmina walked toward the bedroom. Her stomach tightened with apprehension.

"Are you all right? You are pale," Isabel asked, studying her. "Wedding jitters," she proclaimed.

"How old are you?" Wilhelmina changed the subject. "You should be preparing to marry soon as well, right?"

Isabel shook her head. "I'm eighteen. Papa says I can

wait as long as I want to get married. I'm going to get married when the perfect man comes along."

"So no one interests you yet?" Wilhelmina wondered how things would be if she'd grown up there. "With so many men about?"

With a dainty shrug, Isabel rushed ahead of her and lifted a small bunch of yellow flowers with netting. "I made this for you. The flowers are made of paper. My mother showed me how to make them. It will be beautiful in your hair."

Her eyes welled at the only wedding gift she'd receive and Wilhelmina reached for it. "How beautiful. Your mother must have been a dear woman."

"Oh, she was." Isabel smiled. "I am so grateful for the time I had with her. She died almost three years ago now and I miss her daily."

Wilhelmina walked into the bedroom and sat on a small bench facing the vanity. "I don't require any help, Isabel. Honestly, I plan to wear this dress and other than pining this to my hair, I am ready."

Wilhelmina studied her reflection after Isabel helped pin the flowers in her hair and went to her own room to change. Fear and anxiety radiated in the light brown eyes that met hers. Her hand trembled when she pushed back an errant lock of hair. This would have been a perfect time for a bit of brandy.

Many times she and Aurora had planned their wedding days. Every scenario had included prolonged discussions of what they'd wear, hairstyle, shoes and the wedding party.

When a knock sounded, she jumped and dropped the brush. "Come in." Her voice was shaky, making her clear her throat. "Please come in."

Isabel peeked in and smiled. "Marcus is here and so are two witnesses. Are you ready?"

As hard as she tried to stop them, tears welled in her eyes, blurring her vision. Her stomach tumbled and she gulped in air. "I am, just give me a moment."

Isabel gave her a knowing look. "It's going to be fine. You just wait and see."

"I think so, too." Wilhelmina mustered a smile.

"I hope we can continue to visit. I can come to see you and when you're in town, we can meet for tea. I'd like to be friends." Isabel hugged her.

"Yes, I would love it as well."

Isabel's warm hand on her arm helped calm her and she let out a breath. "I'm terrified. What if this is all a huge mistake?"

"I can only imagine," Isabel said. "You are so brave to come so far alone and marry someone. However, I am glad you're marrying him. He's a good man. Believe me, I know"

"How could you?" Perhaps in a futile effort to gain a few moments, Wilhelmina asked that question.

A soft smile curved Isabel's lips. "I was recently engaged to a nice man. My father disapproved because he is so much older than me. After much consideration, I broke it off. Shortly thereafter, he married someone else." She sighed. "It proved he didn't love me as much as he declared. Father was right. And Father thinks you two are a good match."

"The right one will come along," Wilhelmina assured Isabel.

"I know. Now let's get your nerves under control."

Wilhelmina nodded. "I am being a silly girl. Nerves have taken over." She closed her eyes and opened them to meet the determined gaze in the mirror. "I'm ready, let's go."

It seemed like only moments later, she stood next to Marcus, flanked by two witnesses. She and Marcus exchanged vows. She recited her vows to love, honor and obey the man until death parted them. Marcus' voice was deep and clear when stating his vows, while hers wavered, at times barely audible.

Marcus stood straight, his gaze moving to her face every so often as if reassuring himself she'd not disappeared. Although outwardly calm, a muscle on his jawline continuously flexed.

Once the pastor proclaimed them husband and wife and announced Marcus should kiss her, Wilhelmina held her breath. Marcus leaned close and pressed a soft kiss to her lips. In spite of the circumstances and it being expected, a heated flush rushed to her face and she wanted to squeeze her eyes shut in mortification at being so juvenile.

Marcus took her hand and led her to where sweet wine was served in small flutes. He pressed her right hand between both of his and whispered into her ear. "I'm nervous, too."

"Really?"

"Of course."

A simple meal of bread, cheese and apples was served along with the sweet wine. The woman, Ann Logan, who'd attended to serve as witness neared and hugged her. "You are the most lovely young lady. I wish you a wonderful life here in Laurel."

"I appreciate you coming without notice to do this." It was nice to meet the friendly woman. "I hope you didn't have to travel too far."

"It is our pleasure. John and I live just around the corner directly behind the chapel. I clean the church and John does any repairs needed. We don't have much to do with our time now that our children have started life on their own. We don't want to be a nuisance and constantly be underfoot."

While she spoke to the woman, her new husband talked with Pastor Ward and Ann's husband. Relaxed and smiling, she noticed he wore the same clothes as the day before. At least he'd shaved and, from the yellowing replacing the purple, his eye and lip had healed considerably in a short time.

Marcus had not unloaded her belongings from the cart, so all she had to do was to fetch her carpetbag. Soon it would be time to leave and head to her new home.

She drank the sweet wine and considered a second drink. Deciding it was best since she'd be out in the cold, Wilhelmina refilled her glass.

Isabel entered the room with a small plate and made a beeline for her. "Nancy and I made a small cake." She lifted the plate. "I hope it's good."

Once the cake was cut and eaten, time had finally arrived to leave.

"Where is your bag? I'll take it outside." Marcus spoke softly, the deep timbre of his voice sent a pulse through her.

"It's in the guest bedroom on the bed," Wilhelmina replied, shyness taking over at his intense scrutiny. "Thank you."

Once goodbyes and hugs were exchanged, Marcus assisted her onto the wagon.

He ensured she was settled, bundled in blankets. He even asked if she'd prefer to sit in the back where she'd be blocked from the wind.

"I think I'll be fine next to you on the bench," Wilhelmina replied, studying the wagon and not sure either place would offer much warmth. Although the front did have overhead protection from rainfall, it was still open to the elements.

Once seated with wrapped warm bricks at her feet, Wilhelmina was comfortable enough.

As they continued on the road, Wilhelmina stole glances at her new husband every so often. When both looked to each other at the same time, he gave her a crooked grin, which exposed a chipped tooth on the upper right side. She couldn't help but smile in return in finding at least one thing not perfect about his attractiveness. She was beginning to think the man wasn't real.

"Why do you fight?"

At the question, both of eyebrows disappeared under his hat. "I suppose it's an easy way to settle an argument. Not the best way, but when it comes to the way of life here, sometimes, it's often expected."

"What was this particular argument about?" Wilhelmina figured he wouldn't answer, but was curious to see how he handled the question.

A soft blush colored his cheeks and he swallowed visibly. "I'd rather not tell you of conversations that transpire in such a place."

It was much too entertaining to allow the subject to drop, so Wilhelmina nudged him. "I know you were in such a place when coming to see about me."

He slid a look toward her. "I apologize again for my recklessness. Al and I fought over his treatment of one of the girls."

"Did you protest out of chivalry or jealousy?"

This time he turned to her, mouth open. "You don't mince words. I protested because no one should mistreat a woman no matter what she does for a living."

It was a good reply, so she let the subject drop. "It's beautiful out here."

Although most of the trees had lost their leaves, the contrast of them with the evergreens made for a beautiful landscape. Wilhelmina yawned, hoping she'd be able to stay awake for the rest of the journey to her new home.

"This is where my family's land begins." There was pride in Marcus' voice as he spoke. "Several generations have lived here."

Wilhelmina jerked upright at the sound of his voice, realizing she'd dozed off on his shoulder.

Her eyes widened at seeing the beautiful surroundings. Snowcapped mountains flanked the horizon while plush green fields stretched as far as she could see. Tall pine trees reached for the skies, which at the moment were a bright blue and cloudless. The land was flat with a clear winding road along the tree edge.

There were no buildings as far as she could tell, so she leaned forward and scanned once again. "Where is your home?"

"Just around the pass there," he said motioning toward the left. Still, she could not see anything.

"It's picturesque here. Very cold." She shivered and pulled her coat tighter.

Suddenly awkward at being so close to him, hips touching, she shifted to the right only to be jostled back against him by the motion of the wagon. Giving up, she relaxed and let out a breath.

They rode in silence for another while before she had to question him again. "Are we still on your lands?"

"Yes, almost to the house, look." He pointed to the left and before her was a large clearing. There were herds of cattle grazing and horses in corrals. A large log ranch house sat centered on the property. Just behind it were two other large buildings she guessed were a stable and a bunkhouse. She spotted chickens running loose and pigs in pens.

Past the house were several men on horseback herding cattle. And just past them, she saw another house.

"The house up there on the hill is ours," he told her matter-of-factly. "My brother, Tobias, and ranch hand, Owen Blake, are the two on horseback. Owen lives up a ways, but he spends some nights in the bunkhouse since it guarantees him a hot meal. Mama and Eleanor, my sister, are great cooks."

She nodded and her stomach tumbled at the thought of meeting his family. "Is that large house your parents' home then?"

"Yes. My sister, Eleanor, brother and James, my brother-in-law, lives there as well. Eleanor and James moved in when Mama got sick."

Before she could inquire as to his mother's health, he continued talking. It was obvious he was excited to share about his family with her. "My brother is also building a house closer to a river that runs behind the tree line."

The closer they got to the house, the more nervous she became. "Will we be staying at our house after today?"

"No. We will be staying at the big house for a week. I'll take you to our house so you can see it and tell me what you wish made or purchased. I have to get the bed finished and you and Eleanor can stuff the mattress. Back here in the wagon, I've put everything that was delivered to the mercantile just a few days ago."

Stuffing a mattress? Wilhelmina looked to the large parcels in the back of the wagon and bit her bottom lip. "Don't you have help to do those kinds of things?"

"Help?"

"Yes, people who work for you."

His wide shoulders lifted and lowered. "We hire ranch hands during the spring and late summer. Several stay all year round, like Owen. A woman comes and helps around the house when Eleanor sends for her."

Wilhelmina had no idea what he meant. She'd never lived without help. In Philadelphia, maids took care of laundry, sewing and cooking. It would be tedious, but she looked forward to interviewing candidates for her new household.

Feeling a bit better, she ensured a pleasant expression as they pulled up in front of the house. A woman came out and stood on the porch and waved.

Just as she lifted her hand to wave back, her husband spoke.

"I'm sure you'll be fine handling our household. It's smaller than this one and you'll only have to cook and clean for the two of us for now and look after a few animals."

Her blood froze.

"I will be doing all that myself?"

"Of course."

She'd never cooked a meal in her life. Lady Price had not fully explained the expectations. Or had she?

Wilhelmina fought hard against the sudden urge to get sick.

# Chapter Eight

Eleanor greeted them, her gaze lingering over Wilhelmina approvingly. Upon reaching the threshold to the family home, Marcus allowed his sister and Wilhelmina to enter before him. It was gratifying to see Tobias' eyes widen at seeing the breathtaking beauty.

Eleanor spoke first. "Hello, welcome, I'm Eleanor, Marcus' sister." She embraced Wilhelmina. "I'm so excited you're finally here. Please sit down, you must be utterly exhausted."

Marcus introduced Tobias, who'd stood upon their entrance. Marcus guided her by the elbow to a sofa just as his parents entered the room. Immediately, his mother looked to his face and scowled. Fortunately, she didn't question his bruising. Instead, she went to her new daughter-in-law with measured, steady steps.

"Welcome to the family, darling. I hope the long journey across the country and then from Laurel out here wasn't too taxing. Thankfully, it's not snowing. It would've taken longer."

"I have to admit it has been a long trip. But thankfully, I won't have to go anywhere for a little while, I hope."

After a pointed look from her mother, Eleanor went to the kitchen. "I'll get some coffee made."

They settled into chairs. Immediately, his mother began peppering Wilhelmina with questions about her life back east. "Did you live in the city?"

"Yes. My family and I own a townhome a few blocks from Logan Square, the largest park in the city center. We often went for carriage rides or walks there during the day."

The room was silent for a beat. Eleanor came from the kitchen. "Did you attend many social events?"

Wilhelmina seemed to ponder how to respond. "My family receives many invitations for parties and balls. Especially during the spring and winter social season."

Eleanor sat down, seeming to forget about the coffee. "Please tell me, err...I mean, us, about the latest fashions. What are the women wearing now? The men, do they wear cravats and top hats?"

Wilhelmina smiled at Eleanor. "Of course they do. My stepsister, stepmother, and I like to sit in the carriage a short distance away upon arriving at social events. Sometimes, we watch for long moments in order to take in the attire of other guests before asking the coachman to go to the front entrance."

Marcus' mother got to her feet and moved toward him. "Excuse me, Wilhelmina, I am going to instruct Marcus and Tobias where your things should go." She pinched his arm and motioned for him to follow her.

It was the fastest he'd seen her move in a long time. Both he and Tobias had to rush to catch up with her just as she walked outside to the porch. She covered her mouth with both hands and looked at him. When she removed her hands, she'd paled. "I think we made a huge mistake."

"What are you talking about?" Tobias asked and then looked to Marcus who shrugged.

"Don't you see?" she said, looking over her shoulder toward the interior. "She's obviously high society. That poor girl won't last one year here in Montana before she'll be demanding to go back home."

It was Marcus' turn to gawk. "What do you mean? I can't send her back, we're married."

"Oh honey. If she can boil water, I'll be shocked. She comes from a life of being pampered. A home with maids and coachmen, for goodness' sake."

Tobias laughed and cupped her elbow as if to escort her back inside. "I'm sure you and Eleanor can teach her, Ma. Don't go getting all upset until you give her a chance."

His mother slapped Tobias' hand away from her arm. "I come from that world, don't you forget it. I wasn't the mistress, but a caretaker in a large home. Although I held a paying position in Virginia where I did some manual work, it was still a very difficult transition for me to come west and have to do everything. Learn to make all those things that I could just walk up the street and purchase. I can't imagine a girl like her, so high born. Oh dear."

All three looked to the door when Eleanor came outside and placed her fists on both hips. "What are the three of you doing out here? Wilhelmina is dead on her feet. I suggest you see her to bed, Marcus, and then you three can chat all you want."

"See her to bed?" He gulped and then bit back a curse when his face warmed up. "What do you mean?"

"Oh for goodness' sake," his mother laughed and pinned both him and Tobias with a look. "Bring the trunks into Marcus' room. We've cleaned it up and made room for her things."

Tobias lifted a chest and went inside. Marcus followed and stopped when his mother spoke again. "Once you escort her to your room, take warm water for her to wash up. Then allow her privacy to sleep for a few hours."


Wilhelmina smiled awkwardly at Jacob Hamilton. The man drank his coffee and seemed content to not say anything. "I hope I didn't bring too much. It seems to be taking a long time for them to carry my things in."

"They are probably talking about you. Nothing bad, just excited at my eldest having him a wife."

"Oh." Unsure what to think, she drank the overly strong coffee. She wondered what would be expected of her this day. It was early evening. Too early to sleep but, at the same time, she yearned to lie upon a mattress and do just that.

"I'll show you to the bedroom." Marcus appeared suddenly, a strange look on his face as he waited for her to stand.

He guided her out of the room and down a short hallway. He opened a door on the right side to a compact bedroom. "This is my bedroom. We'll stay here for a few days until our own bed, table and chairs are done. I'll get you some hot water to freshen up and you should lie down and rest for a few hours."

She wanted to weep with relief. "That sounds wonderful. Thank you so much."

When he shifted and didn't move, Wilhelmina understood. It would awkward, at best, these first few days. She neared and kissed his cheek. "Thank you for everything."

His warm smiled made her stomach do funny things. "I appreciate you coming all this way. Let me get that water."

The room was well appointed, with a large bed, wardrobe and washbasin stand. There were also a small table and chair next to a window. Wilhelmina was pleasantly surprised to find the décor tasteful and although masculine, the addition of a small landscape sketching over the bed softened the space.

Once she washed up and donned a fresh shift, Wilhelmina climbed into the freshly made bed and, without a moment's hesitation, fell into an exhausted slumber.

A soft sound woke Wilhelmina. With wide eyes, she attempted to see in the dim surroundings. Once again, she heard the snore and turned to her left. Her husband was fast asleep. At least, she assumed it was her husband who slept so soundly.

The sun had either just set or was rising, it was hard to tell which. Either way, she'd slept much too long. Straining to hear any noise outside, she could not make out any sounds of movement. Perhaps, it was early morning.

Could it be she'd slept from the late day through the entire night? Unable to stop herself, Wilhelmina turned left and studied her new husband's face. Marcus was handsome and large, his frame taking up a fair portion of the bed. He lay, fully dressed, atop the blankets. One hand was under his head, the other rested on his thigh.

Soon, she'd know him intimately. They'd be husband and wife for the rest of their lives. The idea gave her pause.

Interesting where fate had led her. Far away from her home, wed to a total stranger and now living with a family she'd otherwise never meet.

Letting out a sigh, she closed her eyes and allowed the sounds of Marcus' breathing to lull her back to slumber.

The next time Wilhelmina awakened, it was to catch a glimpse of Marcus washing up from a basin in the bedroom.

He'd removed his shirt and used a cloth to perform his morning routine. Humming under his breath, he dipped the washcloth back into the water and ran it over his chest. The man was quite breathtaking.

It was the first time she'd seen a male up close, bereft of a shirt. And although inappropriate, she kept her breathing even and eyes half-closed so she could keep watching.

When he hesitated and looked to the bed, she purposely breathed heavier, pretending deep sleep.

Finally, Marcus finished and pulled on a clean shirt. He moved closer to the bed and reached out to her. His hand was heavy on her shoulder, yet it brought an involuntary shudder.

"Wilhelmina. It's time to wake up," he whispered.

She opened her eyes and met his darkened hazel ones. "Good morning."

He gave her a fast nod. "I'll give you privacy. There's fresh water in the pitcher. My sister, Eleanor, has started breakfast."

"Will you be in the kitchen?" Wilhelmina did not want to attend breakfast alone without him. "Should I meet you there?"

"Yes, ma'am. I'll be there." He walked out of the bedroom, closing the door behind him.

Wilhelmina looked up to the ceiling. It would be the first day of her new life. While terrified, a thrill of excitement floated along the edges.

After dressing, Wilhelmina made her way to the dining room. Every face surrounding the table turned to her.

Prompted by the clearing of Eleanor's throat, the men stood awkwardly, as if not used to the actions of polite society.

"Good morning," Wilhelmina said, her voice shaky. "I'm sorry to be late. What time do you breakfast? I will ensure to be on time after today."

Everyone looked to one another. Finally, Eleanor spoke. "We don't have a set time. We eat when the food is ready. If you'd like to help, I am usually in the kitchen by sun up." She noticed the matriarch of the family was missing from the meal, but decided not to ask about her just yet.

"Help?" Wilhelmina looked toward the kitchen. There was no one about. Were there no servants? "Yes...of course."

Unsure what to do, she followed Eleanor to the kitchen. "Is there hot water for tea?"

"Yes." Her new sister-in-law smiled broadly. "Like you, I prefer it over the bitterness of coffee. Especially in the morning."

"I don't think I could ever get used to coffee. I like the

75

smell of it, however." She poured tea and waited to see what Eleanor would do next.

With expert precision, her new sister-in-law broke two eggs into a frying pan. She slid bread onto the heated flat surface of the stove turning it once it browned. After sliding the eggs next to several slices of bacon, she placed the bread onto the plate. "I'll carry it for you so you don't spill your tea."

Once seated, the conversation mostly centered on what the men planned to do that day. It seemed they were moving a herd of cattle from one pasture to another and separating some calves from their mothers. The action seemed inhumane to Wilhelmina, but she didn't comment.

Marcus remained attentive, ensuring she had butter nearby for her bread, and even poured cream into her tea. He seemed distracted at the prospect of getting someone to help him with making furniture that afternoon.

After a brisk knock, the door opened and another man entered. Tall like the Hamiltons, he was, however, lighter of skin, bearded and spoke in short gruff sentences. "The ranch hands are here." His light brown eyes flicked to Wilhelmina, but then he promptly ignored her.

No introductions were made and she could barely restrain from doing so. She looked to Eleanor whose warm gaze fell upon the man. "Wilhelmina, this is my husband, James. He's a bit on the rough side."

The man looked to her and nodded. Moments later, Marcus and Tobias left with James. The patriarch of the family headed to where she presumed was the bedroom he shared with his wife.

"Why didn't your husband join us for breakfast?"

"He ate earlier. Had to go meet the new ranch hands. There is much to get done before winter hits. Once the snow begins to fall, we will be homebound."

Wilhelmina considered what her sister-in-law said. "Do you think I will be in my own home by then?"

"Oh yes. In a couple days. Which reminds me. We have to get your larder fully stocked. Once we knew of your upcoming arrival, Mother and I made a list for Marcus. He went to town and got everything. It's at the house."

"Where is your mother this morning?"

Eleanor's face softened. "Mother is unwell most days. I take her breakfast to the bedroom."

"You do all this by yourself?" Wilhelmina couldn't believe there wasn't at least one servant to assist.

"Mostly, yes." Eleanor sipped from her tea. "A few days a week, a local woman comes in the afternoons to help. She also cleans the boys' bedrooms and does laundry. Mildred is a godsend. She lives nearby with her husband and son."

The news made Wilhelmina feel a bit better. "I will hire someone as well. Is it hard to find live-in help?"

There was an awkward silence that stretched until, finally, Eleanor let out a long breath. "For a household of two, it is rare that anyone hires help. There are precious few women able to get away from their own duties to work. Mildred does so only because they need the money. Her husband is ill and can only manage light work and her son is much too young to work."

Eleanor considered her next words carefully. "All you have to do is cook, clean and laundry for two people. In the spring keep a garden."

"It's just that..." she was interrupted when, once again, the door open. Marcus returned. On his heels was a black dog. It rushed to Wilhelmina, who let out a yelp at the exuberant dog's advance.

Her husband smiled and lowered down to wrap an arm around the dog. His hazel eyes were bright upon meeting hers and, once again, the fluttering in her stomach commenced. "This is Buck. My dog. He'll be living with us." There was pride in his voice and he hugged the dog closer. "Buck, say hello."

The dog lifted a paw and placed it on Wilhelmina's leg

then gave a short bark. She chuckled at the antics. "Nice to meet you as well, Buck."

"I've got a couple men helping with the furniture. Tables and chairs will be done today. I'll need you to come and tell me where you want shelves and such."

Before she could reply, Eleanor interjected. "The mattress cover is done. Wilhelmina and I will stuff it this afternoon." She looked to Wilhelmina. "We may as well get this all cleaned up. Much to get done today." She piled the plates into a tall stack and carried them toward the kitchen. "Be a dear and get the rest, please."

Wilhelmina looked to Marcus, wondering if Eleanor spoke to him or her. When he didn't move to do anything, she stood. "I will see you this afternoon then."

His lips curved. "Yes." Her husband leaned forward and kissed her on the lips. Caught off guard, her eyes widened.

Whistling, he left the house, Buck at his side. Both seeming excited at the prospect of going out into the bitter cold.

Wilhelmina followed Eleanor's instructions as to what to do. Once the dishes were done, which included several trips to a water pump and emptying out of dirty water by the bucketful, they cleaned both the kitchen surfaces and the table.

Eleanor swept the kitchen floor after instructing Wilhelmina to lay a fresh tablecloth and vase of flowers on the dining table.

Interestingly, the work made the morning go by quickly. Where she'd dawdled about the house sometimes reading, other times absently stitching, the act of moving about taking care of chores was quite satisfying.

"I am going to make the bed and check on Mother. You can tidy up yours, as well."

"Is your mother very ill?" Wilhelmina finally asked.

"She is," Eleanor replied and let out a long sigh. "She really isn't well at all. The doctor has tried many things, but none have worked. On good days, she can get out of bed. But most days she remains in her bedroom. I am not sure how much longer she can withstand living in so much pain. Mostly stomach pains that make her cry out."

"My friend's mother suffered from stomach ailments. But after taking a new treatment, she has done remarkably well. I will write her right away and find out what she was prescribed."

Eleanor's face brightened. "That would be wonderful. However, it's hard to get mail once winter hits."

All the talk of winter worried Wilhelmina. It sounded as if the winters were going to be harsh. She'd always had a warm house. And although it snowed in Pennsylvania, at times quite a bit, it was rare to be stranded for days.

Back in the bedroom, she arranged the bed linens. Since she'd only be there for a couple of days, Wilhelmina unpacked one more dress, a serviceable travel ensemble in muted tones. She'd brought plenty of housedresses, but after seeing what Eleanor wore, they seemed too frilly for Montana.

As soon as possible, she'd visit a seamstress in town and order a new wardrobe more suitable to her new lifestyle. She stood by the door and scanned the tidy room and smiled. Perhaps life here would be good for her. For some strange reason, the steady work gave her a sense of accomplishment and pride.

A giggle escaped at her thoughts. Her life had certainly changed and, after a very odd set of circumstances, she found it hard not to smile. She was married to a handsome stranger, performing domestic duties and about to go see about a new home and make a mattress.

Wilhelmina decided to speak to Eleanor and ask for cooking and cleaning lessons. Not only had Wilhelmina never cooked, but she'd not washed clothes, swept, nor had she ever in her life expected to do so. Her gardening experience was limited to flowers and, even that, she only did rarely during spring days when boredom took over.

The ride to her new home was short. It only took, perhaps, ten minutes to get there as Eleanor kept the horse that pulled the wagon they'd climbed onto at a leisurely pace. Her sister-in-law expertly handled the reins while pointing to certain areas and explaining what type of berries, herbs and such could be harvested.

Wilhelmina felt as if she should be holding a pen and paper to take notes and make graphs. Her head swam with all the information she'd memorized since rising that morning.

It was all she could do to remember how eggs were cooked besides how to clean up and sweep. Then there was the daunting task of water pumping and disposal.

It would be an understatement to say she was overwhelmed at the prospect of running a household entirely on her own.

"I'm afraid I must tell you, this is so much more than I expected. The ad stated a man of means, which I understood to imply money and a comfortable lifestyle. All of these duties, as much as I have not minded doing them, may prove too much for me."

Eleanor nodded. "I suspected as much. It is my fault. Marcus is financially comfortable. He has money in the bank and owns a large amount of land and part of the herd. And believe me, he can afford for the both of you to have hired help. It's just that it will be hard to find someone in these parts. Also, once winter comes, traveling is almost impossible."

"What will I do? I don't know the first thing about churning butter or killing a chicken. I heard you mention you'd be making chicken for supper and asked the men to bring two chickens."

When Eleanor laughed, her joy was infectious and

Wilhelmina smiled in return. "They will bring the chickens already beheaded and without feathers. The ranch hands do that for me, which I appreciate. Let's convince Marcus to extend your stay for a few days. I will teach you the basics. The rest I can help you with."

Feeling better, Wilhelmina looked to the surrounding area noting the beauty of the landscape.

One thing was for sure. Her new home was quite beautiful.

The beauty of it, however, did little to ease her sense of trepidation.

# Chapter Nine

What was to be her new home was a smaller replica of Marcus' parents' house. Wilhelmina was pleasantly surprised, having expected something akin to the more primitive homes they'd passed the day before when traveling from town. Especially since Marcus had explained he'd built it with help of local men.

In the distance, there were a couple of smaller homes. Eleanor explained that they belonged to local ranch workers who had family. Those without family to support preferred to live in bunkhouses and work for their room, board and meals.

"How many ranch hands does Marcus have?" she asked, pondering how to climb down from the high bench once they stopped.

"Pa and he share ten men. My husband and I own land just over that ridge. But since Mother's been ill, we've lived at my parents' house so I can take care of her."

"Who will be with her today?"

"She assured me she felt well enough. I imagine Pa will stop in every so often. We won't be longer than a few hours. Once we unload and set up the pantry and such, we'll only work on the mattress for a couple hours. Should be back in plenty of time to start supper." She gave Wilhelmina a bright smile. "Your first cooking lesson."

"Thank you so much. I am so grateful you are here. Otherwise, I'd be lost and probably returned home by Marcus."

"I doubt that very much," Eleanor said, pulling the wagon to a stop. She pulled on a wooden brake and swiftly climbed down.

Wilhelmina was a bit slower, gingerly avoiding falling on her bottom.

Eleanor handed her an armful of fabric. "It will take us a couple trips to get all this inside."

It took four trips. After putting things away and setting up to stuff the mattress, Wilhelmina's arms and lower back ached as she watched Eleanor open the windows and rush to the back of the home.

There was one chair and, not caring if Eleanor balked, Wilhelmina collapsed upon it. It was late morning and there was still so much to be done. How would she endure?

"Marcus did a wonderful job. This is only my second visit to the house. It's larger than I expected." Eleanor went to the kitchen and began jamming wood into the stove. "Need to warm it up a bit, don't you think?"

"How do you do it?" Wilhelmina fought the urge to cry. "I am already drained of energy."


Eleanor looked to her and let out a breath. "I suppose you'll get used to it. I was born here, so I've spent all my life doing these things and constantly working. Don't worry, you'll be fine."

Fine, indeed. Somehow, Wilhelmina doubted she'd ever be able to keep up with her sister-in-law.

Unable to keep curiosity at bay and despite weariness, Wilhelmina explored her new home.

As Eleanor stated, the house was quite nice, although very different from her family home. Thick tree trunks formed sturdy walls. There was a large front room, which she assumed would be partly a dining area. The kitchen was spacious and open. There were two bedrooms, both the same size, and a small privy between them. Next to the kitchen there was an impressive larder, which was almost fully stocked and a tiny room, which she figured could be made into a sewing room or perhaps a library. She looked around wondering if people had libraries there in the west.

When she walked back to the front, Eleanor stood in the kitchen with both hands on her hips looking up at a wall. "You'll need shelves put up here. There, as well." She pointed to the opposite all. "The larder is well enough completed, don't you think?"

"I agree," Wilhelmina said, already imagining herself cooking in there

"Why don't we make tea and begin the task of storing the items we brought?"

They spent the next few hours stuffing the mattress from large bales of cotton. Wilhelmina's arms burned from the work but, thankfully, Eleanor kept her distracted by telling her stories of growing up in Laurel and answering all her questions regarding housekeeping.

Finally, the task completed, Eleanor announced it was time to return to the large house to rest for a bit before starting supper.

Mind awhirl, Wilhelmina wearily climbed into the wagon seat allowing Eleanor to see about the horse. She watched to ensure to get familiar with the process, but was much too exhausted to assist.

Eleanor climbed up onto the seat and let out a breath. "Let's go to the house. I'll check on Mother and make sure she eats a bit. You can take a rest. I'll wake you up in time to fix dinner."

"I can't believe how well you seem to read my mind. I will certainly require rest before being of any help."

With a side-glance at her, Eleanor giggled. "I don't want you to be too overly tired for your first true night of marriage. It will be understandable if you are not up early tomorrow morning."

Heat rose to her cheeks and she let out a sigh. "I'm not sure I'll be prepared for that either." She'd not thought about what the night would bring. Marcus would expect the marriage to be consummated.

Wilhelmina closed her eyes. "Oh goodness."

Eleanor hugged her and let out a sigh. "I'm so happy to see Marcus married to such a pretty and nice lady." It seemed her sister-in-law didn't worry overmuch about what the night would bring. "I expect to see you glowing in the morning."

When Wilhelmina covered her face, Eleanor laughed and urged the horses towards home.


By the time supper was over and Wilhelmina was able to retire to the bedroom to prepare for bed, she could barely stand. The thought of what was to come, however, kept her very much alert. It would not do at all to be too tired to remember her wedding night. The first night she became a real woman was something she wanted to commit to memory.

While brushing out her hair, Marcus entered the room. She felt silly at the now familiar fluttering in her stomach. He came up to where she sat and stood behind her. "You have beautiful hair."

"Thank you." Her breath caught when he swept her hair aside and pressed a kiss to the juncture of her neck and shoulder. Shivers traveled down her spine at the warm lips touching her skin. He smelled clean, freshly bathed. It was then she noticed the damp curls that touched his collar.

In the mirror, she watched him dispense of his clothing, not seeming at all abashed that she could see him. He went to the bed and pulled back the sheets. When he turned and met her gaze in the mirror, the normally light hazel eyes were dark with promise.

"Come to bed, Wife." He stood by the bed, waiting for

her to come to him. He was not hurrying her but, at the same time, the idea of what would occur shook her until Wilhelmina wasn't sure standing was possible.

Of course, she'd been told what transpired between a man and a woman in the marriage bed. She and Aurora had many a talk on the subject between giggles and wrinkling of noses. The entire business seemed so brash and, frankly, rudimentary. Yet seeing him unclothed except for underwear, she actually wanted to touch him and be touched by the handsome man.

It was a wonder the brush in her hand didn't break in half by the strength of her grasp on its handle. Wilhelmina took in a shaky breath and placed it down on the dresser top, then stood to remove her robe.

Before he could touch her, she hurriedly rushed to slide between the sheets and pulled them up to cover her chest. She watched wide-eyed as Marcus pulled his bottoms off. His manhood was so different than what she expected. Unable to look away, she studied his nudity with interest. She was shocked by how fast her breathing became.

When he came to lie next to her, she froze, panicked at knowing any moment now, he'd mount her. And the part of him she'd thought much too large to fit, in any form, would be driven into her body.

Wilhelmina let out an involuntary yelp when Marcus leaned over her. His chuckle made her scowl up at him. "No need to make fun of me. I don't think it's very gentlemanly of you to do so."

"You're scared of what is about to happen. I apologize." Sounding not at all apologetic, he pressed a kiss on her lips. "Relax, I will go slow and give you time."

His touch was soft, the press of his body against hers ever so perfect. He deepened the next kiss and she found herself not wanting him to stop.

Instead of pushing away as she'd hoped not to do, she clung to his shoulders, never wishing their closeness to end.

Minutes later, the room and everything in the

surroundings disappeared as Wilhelmina became lost in the caresses and sounds of their lovemaking.

At one point, she wished him to move faster, to take her fully and end the fervent need boiling inside. At the same time, she expected it would be a painful union of their bodies the first time.

The piercing did, in fact, hurt. But she was so lost in him, so needing of whatever it was that eluded her, that Wilhelmina's pushed past it.

Marcus took her to heights she'd never thought existed to the point the pain was forgotten.

Mouth over hers, he swallowed her exclamations, ensuring the others in the household did not hear.

When Marcus' movements hastened, all rhythm lost, Wilhelmina, too, lost control and dug her nails into his back. Marcus shuddered in what she assumed was the culmination of lovemaking for a man. When he lay spent over her, Wilhelmina slid her palms up and down his back.

The sounds of their heavy breathing were the last things Wilhelmina heard. Unable to stay awake any longer, her head on her husband's chest, she fell into a deep sleep.

Morning came too soon. Wilhelmina stretched like a cat in the sun and instantly realized she was in bed alone. She'd hoped to greet the family alongside Marcus, but it seemed he'd risen early by the lack of warmth on his side of the bed.

She was mortified at facing the family, as they'd, no doubt, know what exactly had transpired between her and her husband. Wilhelmina remained a bit longer, unsure what the day would bring.

"Did you sleep well?" Eleanor's question was, of course, laden with mischief. The twinkle in her eyes since he'd entered the room made Marcus roll his own.

He gave his sister a droll look only to gain a pointed one in return. "Yes, thank you for asking."

His mother was absent from breakfast again and his chest constricted at her attending family meals less and less often. Tight lines around his father's mouth made him hesitate to ask how she fared. Instead, he'd ask Eleanor once they were alone.

Tobias reached for a biscuit, his eyes trained on Marcus. "When are you moving into your house?"

As much as Marcus wanted to live with Wilhelmina and start their new life, a part of him dreaded not being around his mother in what could prove to be her last days. Over the last few months, she'd become weaker and had aged until barely recognizable. There was no doubt in his mind she was in a great deal of pain, going from one day to the next in a fog from high doses of laudanum and opium his father procured for her.

"Next week. We need to get settled before winter fully sets in." His mind instantly went to spending long, cold nights and days with Wilhelmina. She'd surprised him by her passionate acceptance of their lovemaking.

Although tentative at first, he'd not had to hold back. His lips curved only to gain him a cough from Eleanor who looked past him to the doorway.

He stood along with his father and brother as Wilhelmina made her way to the table. "Good morning. I apologize for my lateness."

"No need, of course," Eleanor replied. "I'll get your breakfast."

"Please, allow me. I can do it." His bride avoided looking at anyone. When Tobias grinned widely, Marcus kicked him under the table.

When his brother yelped in pain, Eleanor laughed. "That's what you get."

When Wilhelmina and Eleanor returned and sat, there was an awkward silence.

Marcus leaned forward and kissed her cheek. "I'm

sure Eleanor will have plenty for you to do here today."

His wife looked to Eleanor. "I have so much to learn."

Everyone ate in silence. Finally, Marcus had to ask. "Pa, how is Mother doing today?"

Jacob Hamilton was the strongest man Marcus knew. At only forty-seven, he seemed too young to be his father. The fact his mother and father married at only sixteen made him wonder how they'd been so fortunate to find true love at such a tender age.

His father's eyes, identical to his, lifted only to look back to the plate. "She's not well at all. I plan to ask Evan Jones to come and check on her."

"I'll go fetch him," James, Eleanor's husband, volunteered. "I'd like to see what's new over at Clover Ranch." He referred to his own family, which consisted of several siblings and two quite austere parents. Marcus often wondered if the reason James rarely showed any emotion was due to his upbringing.

His sister's wedding had been devoid of more than stilted conversation and no music whatsoever as James' mother insisted it would be sinful.

Marcus had laughed at how often his sister sang while cooking. James always looked on with the closest he could come to a smile and warmth in his gaze. It always assured him to know how much James loved Eleanor.

The large man stood. "Is there anything else anyone would like me to get?"

Wilhelmina looked to Marcus before speaking. "If I may ask," she said in a quiet voice. "I have two letters to mail."

"Of course," James replied with a nod. "Anyone else?"

Eleanor smiled at her husband. "Pick me up some peppermint and tea."

Once James left, Tobias and Jacob followed suit.

Eleanor, not seeming in any hurry to leave the table, lifted her cup of tea and sipped. She looked toward the hallway and then to him. "Mother is not well at all. I think we should prepare ourselves." Her whisper was hoarse with emotion. "She's refused to eat for three days now. I haven't told Pa about it. I have tried to get her to drink some broth, but that is all she will have."

The tightness in his chest brought moisture to his eyes and he closed them tightly. "Evan will help. He is a good doctor."

"What, exactly, ails your mother?" Wilhelmina asked, covering his hand with hers. "Is there anything I can do?"

"We don't exactly know," Eleanor said. "It started as aches and pains, then her stomach constantly cramped. At first we tried all sorts of tonics hoping it would pass, but she got progressively worse. So we called for Dr. Jones to examine her." Eleanor stopped talking, too choked up.

The warmth of her hand strengthened Marcus. "It's stomach cancer."

"Oh no," Wilhelmina replied after a soft gasp. "That is horrible. She must be in great pain." She pushed her barely eaten breakfast away. "I will go find some herbs and make some tonic that will sooth her stomach. Will you accompany me?" She looked to Eleanor.

"No, Marcus can go with you. I will see about cleaning up. Thank you for doing this. Anything that helps her feel better is appreciated."

Marcus gave his sister a grateful nod when Wilhelmina reached for her cup of tea and Eleanor responded with a saucy wink.


Although the air was brisk and the breeze quite strong, it didn't cool Wilhelmina's heated face. She'd not wanted time alone with Marcus just yet. She wasn't prepared for any kind of normal conversation, as her heart couldn't seem to settle in his presence. Yet, thankfully, he acted as if he'd not noticed.

He pointed to a crop of trees in the near distance. "Over there is where my mother and sister used to always harvest herbs and such. There was a garden beside the house, but with all the housework and such, Eleanor hasn't the time to keep it up."

"I'll need a basket or something to carry them in." Wilhelmina spoke without meeting his gaze.

When he left, she touched both hands to her face and, sure enough, it was warm. "Darn it," she said out loud, grateful for the cool air.

Once he returned, they walked to the trees. Marcus, seeming in a good mood, hummed.

He turned to her with a smile. "I used play hide and seek here with my brother and sister when we were kids. We often left Tobias for last until he'd give himself away by crying."

"That was quite cruel, poor little boy."

"I agree, it was. However, that poor little boy was quite a handful, constantly in trouble. He once escaped through the window when mother sent him to bed without supper. He then crawled through the front door hoping to make it to the kitchen."

"Did he?" Wilhelmina asked, giggling.

"Almost, but Eleanor caught sight of him and threw her shoe at him." Marcus chuckled, showcasing deep dimples Wilhelmina had only caught glimpses of. Her husband was very attractive and she was grateful for it.

"Pa grabbed him by the scruff of his shirt and held him up but Ma couldn't stop laughing long enough to scold him."

The story told of a close-knit family. Marcus had a good upbringing, unlike hers. Once her mother died, things had changed drastically.

When they reached a shaded area, she scanned the ground for pepper root. Unsure it grew there in Montana, she'd not thought to ask Eleanor.

Marcus crouched down and plucked a young plant and held it up. "Do you have any siblings? Is this something herbal?"

It was hard not to smile at his attempt to pass a weed off as something useful. "I have one stepsister. You shouldn't pluck plants from the ground unless we will use them."

He stared at the weed. "You feel bad for this plant? Maybe we should use it for something."

"It's a dandelion. And yes, parts of it are edible, but you'd need quite a bit to make anything."

Looking her in the eye, he tossed it over his shoulder.

Wilhelmina lifted a brow. "I would say Tobias was not the only naughty boy in the family."

They continued to walk, the discussions going from their pasts to the current weather and what to expect in the coming months. Wilhelmina laughed when Marcus attempted to climb a tree to show her how easy it was only to fail before reaching the first branch.

Heart warm, she realized they were comfortable around one another. No matter how intimate they'd been the night before, her husband ensured she was not left adrift with her feelings.

She was lucky, indeed, and very grateful for him.

"Marcus, thank you for sending for me. I hope I don't disappoint you with my lack of knowledge of homemaking."

When he neared and wrapped his arms around her, Wilhelmina couldn't suppress a smile.

"I'm sure you won't."

# Chapter Ten

Wilhelmina cut potatoes while watching how Eleanor dusted chicken with flour. The woman had a no-nonsense way around the kitchen, remaining on task, her brows pinched in concentration. "Now you do the rest of it."

It was simple to follow directions. She completed the tasks Eleanor set her to in between jotting notes in a journal she'd brought. To think, the book she'd planned to write thoughts in was now going to be her instruction manual for household duties.

At suppertime, Wilhelmina smiled broadly, her chest bursting with pride when placing the finished meal in the center of the table.

"It smells great," Marcus told her and she could only flush and look to Eleanor.

"Your sister did the hard part. She taught me how to make the roasted potatoes. She cooked most of the chicken and made the bread."

Once again, the matriarch of the family was absent from the dinner meal as well as James.

Wilhelmina looked to Marcus' father noting his somber demeanor. "How is Mrs. Hamilton?"

Jacob Hamilton shook his head. "Not well. I'm hoping

James arrives soon with Doctor Jones. Something has to be done."

"I'll check on her," Eleanor said and got up from the table, leaving the four remaining people to eat in silence. Although she noted exchanges of glances between the men, Wilhelmina didn't see fit to comment. It was obvious everyone was worried about their mother.

An hour later, James returned with a sandy-haired, elegant man holding a medicine bag. Evan Jones, the doctor, was much younger than Wilhelmina expected. He appeared to be, perhaps, barely thirty. He removed his hat and nodded in her direction.

Jacob went to the doctor and they spoke in low tones while Tobias and Marcus remained seated, but quiet. When the doctor and Jacob went toward the back, Wilhelmina looked to Marcus. "Is there anything I can do to help?"

"No." He shook his head with a grim expression. "Why don't you get ready for bed? There isn't much more to be done today. Once Evan finishes examining Mother, he will probably have something to eat and spend the night here. Tobias and I will see about it."

Too tired to argue, Wilhelmina prepared for bed and waited for Marcus to join her. She wondered about the repercussions if the doctor pronounced the ill woman would not live much longer.

Although her own mother died when she was young, the pain of losing her returned full force at times.

For Marcus, it would undoubtedly be as hard to accept and deal with.

Through the bedroom window, she spotted James taking horses toward the stables. The sun had dipped below the horizon, elongating the shadows that stretched across the earth.

The view would never tire her. How very different Montana was from Philadelphia. Everything from vegetation to the landscape did not resemble anything

94

she'd seen before. There were mountains in Pennsylvania, but in Montana, they seemed majestic, grander in a way.

Absently, she wondered what her family did at the moment. Slept, probably, as it was later in the east. They thought she'd left to go to Virginia. Instead, she'd boarded the train and debarked at the next station where she transferred to a train headed west. She'd left a note with the Lady Price, asking it be delivered to her father two days after she'd left.

It was probable her stepmother and stepsister were not sorry Wilhelmina had not gone to Virginia. The farther she was, with her scandalous reputation, the better for them is what they'd think.

Although her father would be sad at her decision, they'd distract him by stating how she'd done the most impulsive, irresponsible thing and they should concentrate on keeping it a secret from their society circles.

The two letters she'd sent with James to town were to Aurora and Lady Price. She informed them about marrying Marcus. She'd not asked either to keep it a secret and, hopefully, they wouldn't. It would serve her stepsister right to find out she'd married a handsome man.

The door opened and she turned. Her husband entered and sat down to remove his shoes. He seemed deep in thought. "Evan is still with Ma. He's drinking coffee and waiting to see how the treatment he administered is working."

"Would you like some hot water? I can fetch it." When she reached the doorway, he took her arm.

"I've decided we'll remain here through the winter months. I can't move away right now." Marcus looked at her then away. "We can move in the spring."

"I understand what you must be feeling, but this is a decision we should speak about. Make together." Wilhelmina attempted to keep her temper in check.

"It's for the best."

"You are not listening to me. Why can't we discuss it?

HILDIE MCQUEEN

How are we to have a good marriage if I am not to be included in any major decisions?"

He stood to his full height, whether to intimidate her, she wasn't sure. "This is not up for discussion. Wouldn't you want to be with your father during his last days?"

Both hands flat on his chest, Wilhelmina pushed him back. "I am not intimidated by you. How dare you question my feelings toward my father?"

"I've decided we will remain. Discussion is not needed at this point." Although he spoke softly, he lifted an eyebrow in challenge.

There it was; the temper she'd been expecting. Wilhelmina refused to back down. "I do not agree and I will not be spoken down to by you."

"Why, because you're from high society? Is that going to be your reasoning against me whenever we disagree? That I'm not worthy of you?"

"Don't you dare put words in my mouth." Wilhelmina blinked back angry tears. "I did not refer in any way to my upbringing."

"What do you want me to say? That I will move into our house regardless of what is happening just to make you happy?" His voice rose just a bit and then his jaw clenched.

Of course, she realized at the moment that, perhaps, her argument was without foundation as she would have agreed to remain. But the fact that he didn't ask for her opinion would not do. If there was a lesson she'd learned from her stepmother it was to ensure, inside the home, the marriage should stand on equal footing.

"My happiness is not the concern at the moment. What is my concern is your attitude."

"What?" He scowled and narrowed his eyes.

Wilhelmina lifted her chin and pointed at his face. "There, that. Most disagreeable."

"I don't..."

Knocks sounded on the other side of the door and Marcus yanked it open.

Eleanor looked from one to the other. "I can hear you all the way in the front room. This is not a time to be arguing. I suggest you both calm down and go to sleep. Get some rest and wait until morning to talk."

"I won't be sleeping in here with him." Wilhelmina crossed her arms.

"Fine by me. I'll sleep in the front room," Marcus said and stormed from the room.

Wilhelmina let out a huff. "I'm so sorry. I hope we didn't disturb your mother."

"You didn't." Eleanor seemed unsure how to proceed next. "What happened?"

"To be honest, I'm not quite sure." Wilhelmina ran her hands down her face. "Now, I'm too upset to sleep and want to cry. I am not sure how your brother and I will ever manage."

Eleanor took her by the elbow and guided her to the bed just as tears spilled. "There now, don't fret. I'm sure it's just a misunderstanding."

"He would not listen to me at all." Wilhelmina let out a shaky breath. "I'm so embarrassed I raised my voice at him. I've not screamed at someone in very a long time."

Her sister-in-law chuckled. "If anyone will bring out a temper in people, it's Marcus. I agree he is impatient and quick to anger, but he will never disrespect you or mistreat you. That, I can assure you."

Not knowing her husband well, Wilhelmina didn't comment on Eleanor's statement.

Her sister-in-law squeezed her arm. "I should let you get some rest. In the morning, things will be better, I'm sure."

"Yes, of course. Again, I apologize." Although she agreed, Wilhelmina did not think for a moment the disagreement would be any different by the next day. The challenge in Marcus' expression had unsettled her. Did he expect her to bow to his every whim without some sort of discussion?

It would not do at all. She'd once heard a woman state that at the beginning of a marriage is when roles are set. Wilhelmina decided she'd not back down. Whether or not she won the argument didn't matter. What did matter was that Marcus understood she would not be ignored when it came to decisions affecting them and their future family.

They would battle to see where the other stood. He was testing her and had tried to assert himself in their relationship.

There was going to be a very important lesson in it for both of them. She'd not back down on her belief that major decision would be discussed nor would she allow him to mow over her as if she were a puppet of some sort.

Mind made up, she fell into a fretful sleep. She knew the next day, she'd face her husband for another bout.

One she would not lose.

Marcus paced from one end of the room to the other, stockinged feet thumping on the wooden floor with each step.

In a chair with a book on his lap, Evan read, ignoring him. He knew Marcus enough to wait. Marcus looked to his friend. "Why do woman have to be so contrary?"

Evan lifted a shoulder. "I think they have to stand their ground sometimes. Other times, they just like to argue."

Although they'd been friends for years, Marcus had never spoken to Evan about women. Since Tobias was nowhere to be seen and probably still angry with him, and his father was already in bed, he didn't have anyone to confide in.

"I told Wilhelmina we would remain here until spring since Mother is not well and she argued about it."

After a few moments, Evan lifted his gaze from the book. "What did she say?"

"Something about my face being disagreeable and how she'd not been included in the decision."

"Hmm," Evan said and pinched the bridge of his nose. "Why didn't you ask her opinion?"

"Whatever for?" Marcus sat down and shook his head. "What would she have said that would make me change my mind? It makes no sense."

"Don't ask me. My last relationship ended rather abruptly by her stating I had the most dreadful idea of what courtship consisted of."

Marcus frowned. "That makes no sense. What did you do?"

"Apparently, not enough." Evan seemed unperturbed. He returned to his reading, leaving Marcus to brew over the argument with his new wife. In the morning, he'd not bring up the argument. If anything, he'd eat early and leave before she appeared. It was best to wait until later and then see if she was over whatever it was that angered her.

Marcus walked down the hallway to his parents' bedroom. The door was cracked, so he pushed it open just a bit more and looked in. On the bed, his mother lay fast asleep. Almost unrecognizable with pale drawn skin and hollowed eyes, her thin chest rose and fell in a slow rhythm.

Clutching her hand, his father slept sprawled in a chair, his long legs stretched out onto a footstool. He looked most uncomfortable. Someone, probably Eleanor, had covered him with a blanket.

The room smelled of a mixture of herbs and illness, stale and damp almost. He didn't step inside, but remained at the door. The woman he loved and depended on struggled to live and there wasn't a damn thing he could do about it.

Marcus could not stop the tear that trailed down his cheek. The tightening in his chest made it almost impossible to breathe. Rage and sadness strangled the air out of him. Nothing or no one would pull him away from spending what limited time there was with his mother.

She was much too young to die. There had to be something Evan or someone could do to save her.

Why didn't Wilhelmina understand?

Perhaps, her family wasn't close-knit. She'd mentioned a stepmother and stepsister as well as a father. If her own mother had died while she was very young, it could be the reason she did not understand how he felt.

Could her lack of warmth from family be the reason Wilhelmina fought him on this issue? What had she said exactly?

He was so confused, too overcome by grief to think clearly. Not entirely sure where to sleep, he went to a cabinet in the hallway and yanked out a blanket.

With it wrapped around him, he lay on the rug in front of the fireplace.

"Is there anything to be done for Ma? You need to save her Evan." He didn't look to his friend. Instead, he kept his gaze on the fire.

Evan let out a long breath. "I've researched it. Went to see Emmett in Billings. He once studied under a specialist. I'm sorry, Marcus. I don't think there is much more I can do except ensure she is comfortable."

Unable to speak, Marcus considered Emmett Jones, Evan's older brother. He was a prominent physician in Billings. Hope dimmed. "Thank you for what you are doing."

"No need to thank me." There was rustling as Evan settled on the sofa.

Just as he was falling asleep, Evan chuckled. "Doesn't look promising that with a new wife, you're sleeping on the floor in here. Maybe I'll hold off on matrimony."

"Go to sleep, Evan," Marcus snapped.

# Chapter Eleven

The sunny day did not affect her disposition the next morning. Wilhelmina walked past the dining table with a curt good morning and directly into the kitchen where Eleanor was already preparing breakfast.

"Good morning, Sister," Eleanor greeted cheerfully. "I hope you slept well."

"I did, thank you." She began cracking eggs into a bowl. "I must manage to get up earlier and help you with gathering eggs and such."

"James does it for me. He's an early riser and doesn't want me out and about in the cold."

There was warmth in Eleanor's smile at speaking of her husband and Wilhelmina smiled in return. "You are very lucky to have such a good man to share your life with."

"Oh, I am. I never stop thanking the Lord for him." Eleanor sighed. "You have a good husband, as well, Wilhelmina. Just needs to settle a bit and get used to the idea he's married now."

It was the perfect opportunity to ask for advice. "When you decided to move here to help with your mother, how did you approach James about it? Did he agree right away?"

"It was not easy. I was unsure how to ask him. Finally, one day over dinner, I told him I was tired of maintaining two households. I asked his opinion on what I could do to make things easier. We finally decided to move here temporarily and bring our cattle and livestock over as well." She shook her head. "It was hard to leave our home. I go there at least every other week to dust and check on things. If I don't have time, James goes."

Wilhelmina admired Eleanor's strength and willingness to sacrifice so much for her ailing mother. "That is all I ask for. That Marcus discusses things with me. I am not against remaining here to help. I understand him wanting to be nearby for his mother. I'd do the same. What angered me was the way he presented it, as if I had no say in the matter. Please don't think poorly of me."

Eleanor laughed. "If anything, I'm glad you stood up to him. He needs to learn."

Feeling better, Wilhelmina helped place the food on the table and poured coffee into empty cups. When she looked to where Marcus sat, the chair was empty. She let out a breath.

*Learn, indeed.*


"Don't take out your anger on the cow," Tobias hollered. "If it kicks you, I'll congratulate it."

Marcus tried, once again, to steer the stubborn animal back to the herd. "If you're so good, then why are two on your side back there?" He motioned to behind Tobias where a pair of cows grazed lazily.

"They are taking a meal break. Can't blame them. My stomach is growling."

Instead of a retort, he could only agree. His own was stomach was hollow with hunger since he'd skipped breakfast. One day, his temperament would be the end of him.

Instead of dwelling, he spurred the horse to nudge the

wayward cow back to the herd. It would be another while before the herd would be in the pasture set aside for them.

His father came up alongside. "The ranch hands will be working on hay bales for the next few days. We'll need to see about fortifying the shelter for the cattle."

"It's going to be a bitter winter," Marcus agreed. "You should be home with Ma."

Jacob pulled his collar up. "She kicked me out of the room. Said I was annoying her by hovering." His lips curved. "In a mood today."

It was good to hear his mother was well enough to be annoyed. "We've never had to wonder what she is thinking."

"Sounds like your wife is much like that." His father pressed his lips together to keep from grinning.

Marcus nodded. "True. I don't understand why she got so mad. I told her we were staying at the house through spring and she said we should have discussed it."

"She's right," he father said and rode off.

First Eleanor, now his father was against him. Did no one agree with him? Marcus looked to where Tobias guided the wayward cows back toward the herd. Definitely couldn't count on his brother, the man would agree with Wilhelmina just to spite him.

Unable to stop, Marcus chuckled at recalling the flare of his wife's nostrils and the fire in her eyes when she'd admonished him the night before. There was no arguing with the fact she was a beautiful woman. It was admirable that, although out of her element, Wilhelmina tried to learn what she could from Eleanor. He'd not heard her complain once. The lifestyle change had to be abrupt. Not just the weather and location, but the lack of amenities and such.

He'd watched as she'd studied everything his sister did, mimicking her movements when doing chores most would consider rudimentary. Her brow wrinkled in concentration, she'd cut a pie, pausing ever so slowly to ensure she did it correctly.

Wilhelmina was a high born lady. He'd expected her to balk and demand to return home upon learning she was expected to do household tasks. Instead, she'd immediately taken to shadowing Eleanor and learning.

It occurred to him it would be a good idea to take her to town. That way, she could purchase anything needed to make it through the winter. Perhaps, if he did something for her, she'd not be so angry at him for choosing to remain at the family home.

The horse bucked and he was almost unseated. Tobias laughed and shook his head. "You lost a couple."

His brother rode off and Marcus chased after him. "I'll get them. Go back to whatever you were doing! Tobias, I'm not in the mood for you today."

Behind him, he heard his father call out to them. "If you two get in a fight, I'm going to rope you together and drag you home."

"Don't give in. Stand your ground," Elaine Hamilton said. The frail woman had insisted on sitting in the front room. Wilhelmina and Eleanor bundled her up with warm blankets by the front window so she could look outside.

On chair next to her mother-in-law, Wilhelmina looked up from her mending. "I am so sorry if we disturbed you last night."

"Eleanor told me what the disagreement was about and I happen to agree with you. Marcus has always been such a headstrong boy. The only way for him to learn is for there to be consequences to his actions." A warm smile curved the ill woman's face. "The stories I could tell you."

Mortified, Wilhelmina hurried to assure her. "It's not that I don't agree with remaining here in the house to ensure he is near you. What angered me was that he made a decision with discussing it with me and then informed me as if I were nothing more than a puppet."

"Jacob and I had a few rows in our first weeks of

marriage. In the beginning, most couples have to get to know each other all over again. It's very different to court than to live together. In your case, there wasn't even courting time."

Outside the window, the wind blew, sending what few leaves remained on trees fluttering to the ground. Wilhelmina had to admit, it was a beautiful view. "I must admit that I miss Philadelphia. Not just the city, but my father as well. How did you adjust to coming here?"

For a long moment, Elaine looked out the window, a pensive expression and soft smile on her face. "It was hard. Things were so different back then. The town was barely being established. I came here with my parents after my father accepted a position with the railroad."

"How old were you?"

"Twelve. I was devastated at leaving my friends and cousins behind in Virginia. I remember my mother crying at night as well. It was a trying and very difficult time. My poor father had his hands full with three women. My sister, Mary, was a bit older than me and proved to be the most hysterical of us."

"Oh, are your parents still alive?"

"My mother is, yes. She lives with Mary near Billings. You'll meet her. She usually visits twice a month." Elaine's eyes sparkled with mirth. "Prepare yourself. She is a force to be reckoned with."

"Oh goodness." Wilhelmina laughed.

They sat in companionable silence until Eleanor came into the room from the back of the house. She looked refreshed and rested. Wilhelmina had insisted she go and relax while she cleaned up breakfast and watched over Elaine.

"I'm going to make tea if anyone wants some," Eleanor announced. "I think we should discuss winter preparations and what we need in the way of supplies so we can go to the mercantile this week."

"Good idea," Elaine replied. "It will give Wilhelmina a

chance to see Laurel and meet the Johnstons." She looked to Wilhelmina. "They own the mercantile. Very nice people."

"I'd love to go." Wilhelmina was excited at the prospect of shopping. She needed fabric to make more serviceable dresses. If they were to be homebound for the winter, it would be the perfect time to do so. She looked to Eleanor. "Can you teach me to make dresses? I'm afraid the only things I've ever made are embroidered handkerchiefs and such."

"Of course," Eleanor replied quickly. "It's easy. And it will give us something to do during the long winter."

After tea, Eleanor and Wilhelmina went to the kitchen to begin preparations for supper. They left Elaine to sleep in the chair.

"She has coloring today, seems to be feeling better," Wilhelmina told her sister-in-law.

The long sigh from Eleanor was followed by a sniffle. "Thanks to the tea you brewed and whatever Evan prescribed, yes. However, she grows weaker by the day. Although she tries to put up a strong front, I can see her pain. I am so scared of losing her. Don't know what I'll do. If only the medicine made her better." Eleanor's voice hitched.

"Don't lose hope. You never know."

Eleanor closed her eyes. "Mother was always so full of energy. I overheard her speak of Grandmother. They are...were very much alike. Both are feisty women who do not mince words. Many times, the ranch hands would hide when they saw Mama coming."

"Oh goodness," Wilhelmina said with a chuckle. "I can't wait to meet your grandmother."

Her mind went back to when her own mother died. Being so young, she'd been more confused than anything. As a matter of fact, for a long time, she'd not accepted it, refused to talk about it. Her mother's death was devastating, crippling her ability to deal with emotions for many years. She existed in a state of ambivalence for a long time. It wasn't until well into her teens that, finally, her personality reemerged.

"What do you think?" Eleanor brought her out of her musings, holding up a huge potato. "Doesn't this look like a cloud?"

"Very much so," Eleanor said, studying the huge spud.


The closer it got to the men returning from work, the more nervous she became. If what her mother-in-law said was true and Marcus was stubborn, then, no doubt, he'd continue to be angry with her.

It didn't matter whether he was mad or not. She'd sit down with him and discuss her views on how decisions in a marriage should be handled.

Surely the man would see her point of view.

Footsteps, deep voices and the door opening and closing sounded and Eleanor shook her head. "They are noisier than a herd of cattle." She looked over her shoulder and shouted, "Make sure you wash up before coming in here. I can smell you!"

There were grumblings, more footsteps and the door opening and closing again. Wilhelmina smiled at her sister-in-law. "What do you think they're doing now?"

"If I know them, Tobias and Marcus are out at the rain barrel scooping water and washing up. James went to our bedroom to change clothes and clean his face. And Father has gone back to check on Mother."

When Wilhelmina went to the dining table to set it, both Tobias and Marcus walked through the front door. Both had wet hair and clean faces. They hung jackets on the pegs by the door and looked expectedly toward the table.

Marcus' gaze lifted to hers. He searched her face for a clue as to what she was thinking then looked away.

No greeting. Wilhelmina decided to be the better

person. "Good afternoon. Go ahead and sit down. Supper is just about ready."

The men moved as one toward the table, James appearing from the back. "It smells very good," James said, smiling broadly.

At once, she and Eleanor served the meal, ensuring each man had a large portion.

When Wilhelmina sat down next to Marcus, he looked to her. "How was your day?"

"Quite interesting. I enjoyed speaking with your mother. She gave me a lot of good advice."

His brows came together in a frown and he looked to Eleanor who feigned not noticing, her lips pressed together in an unsuccessful attempt to hide a smile. "You spoke to her?"

"Mother sat out here with us for a good while. She had a good day today," Eleanor announced to the table. "I took her back a few minutes ago as she needed to get some rest."

Marcus cleared his throat. "I am planning to go to town this week. Would you like to go?"

Wilhelmina looked to her sister-in-law. "Oh, that is most timely. Eleanor and I have compiled a list of things we must get. Your mother also has items she'd like purchased. If you can take us, it would be nice."

"Indeed," Eleanor said. "We have to get supplies and ensure the kitchen and house are stocked for winter."

Leaning over his plate, he resumed eating, not speaking to them for the rest of the meal. Wilhelmina almost felt bad as it became obvious he'd meant the invitation to be for her alone. But at the moment, she cared more that he didn't think all was forgotten or would be by his invite alone.

"Can we speak after supper?" she asked him in a soft voice. "I don't believe our discussion from last night is finished."

His jaw clenched, the muscle jumping when he clamped his teeth together. "The matter is settled."

"No it is not."

Everyone around the table stopped eating and watched them with expectation. Wilhelmina refused to back down. "We will speak after supper." She looked to her father-in-law. "Would you like more stew?"

Thankfully, the woman who came on occasion to help, showed up after supper and took over cleaning the kitchen. Wilhelmina walked out to the porch to search for Marcus.

In the distance, she spotted her stubborn husband who'd escaped as soon as he finished eating. Marcus was probably attempting to avoid her. He stood in the center of a corral holding the end of a rope with the other secured around a horse's neck. The animal trotted in a circle as Marcus made clicking sounds and spoke to the animal in soft tones.

She pulled her shawl tight around her shoulders, the fabric barely enough to keep her warm. Then she walked to where he worked.

If he saw her, Marcus did not acknowledge her, but continued with whatever he was doing.

"I feel that a husband and wife should discuss anything that will impact both of them," Wilhelmina called out and leaned on the fence to stare at him.

"Why should we discuss something when a decision is made?" he quipped back, tugging at the rope.

"Because it's what civilized people do."

"I am civilized."

"I am making a point. How would you feel if I decided we'd eat beans every day? I made the decision without asking your opinion and just served them."

"That makes no sense. Why would anyone eat beans every day?" He looked at her with narrowed eyes. "Are you really planning to do that?"

"It's just an example." She resisted the urge to stomp her foot. She shivered, but refused to go back indoors. They'd have a conversation whether he liked beans or not. "You decided where we'd live and didn't give me a choice or an opinion on the matter. At this point, you do not know if I would have thought it a good idea or not. You don't know if I want to be here or not. You did not give me an opportunity to prepare for a very big change in plans."

He walked to the horse and untied the rope. The man's movements fascinated her, his wide back stretching as he reached up to pull the saddle from the animal. With determined, long strides he walked towards her and placed the heavy item on the fence. Marcus' lips remained pressed into a tight line and she could see the stubborn resolve. The man would not give in easily and admit to being wrong, or at least partially understand where she stood.

"I am not going to change my mind. What do you have to say on the matter?"

Wilhelmina could only gawk at him. She bit down, grinding her teeth to keep from screaming. "Is that how you want to start this conversation?"

"We've been talking for a few minutes."

After a fortifying breath, Wilhelmina met his gaze. "Do you understand what I said when I asked that we discuss things before a final decision is made?"

"I'm not an idiot. Yes, I understand, but I don't agree." When he rolled his neck and looked up to the sky as if for patience, Wilhelmina spun on her heel and headed back to the house.

It was no use. The man was as stubborn as a mule. She rushed past the main room to the bedroom and closed the door. Then she fell over the bed, pushed her face into the bedding and screamed.

# Chapter Twelve

The wagon ride to Laurel was entertaining. Tobias and Marcus sat on the bench while Wilhelmina and Eleanor settled into the back of the wagon. Although it was quite cold, blankets and warmed bricks helped a great deal.

Eleanor pointed out several places and told her stories of the people who lived there. Although Wilhelmina and Marcus had yet to speak about things, for the time being she allowed it to pass. It wouldn't do to ruin the day by arguing with her stubborn husband.

Upon arriving in town, the brothers assisted the women down and they were immediately surrounded by several townspeople. It was interesting that most did not try to conceal their curiosity at meeting Wilhelmina.

Two women neared and both hugged Eleanor. Her sister-in-law's face was bright with joy. "Wilhelmina, this is Gladys. She is Evan Jones' nurse." She motioned to the woman who smiled broadly in return and then turned to the other woman who'd stepped out of the building they stood in front of. "And this is Gemina. She and her husband, Howard, own the mercantile."

The women seemed anxious to get her inside to talk.

No doubt, they sought to find out the information every other woman had sought to get from her.

Wilhelmina turned to find Marcus. He watched on with a curve to his lips, obviously at ease since she was not frowning.

Just then an argument broke out across the street and two men began trading punches.

"Not again," Gemina said with a huff. She turned to watch the commotion while Wilhelmina went to stand behind Marcus.

One man fell to the ground. Wilhelmina looked to Marcus. "Who are they?"

"The one standing is Evan's brother, Elias. He's a rancher." Marcus chuckled when the fair-haired Elias fell face first onto the ground because the other man grabbed his legs.

"Isn't anyone going to do something?" Wilhelmina asked just as Gladys rushed over with a bucket of water.

"Cut it out," the woman admonished the fighters and doused them with the cold water. She stormed away, leaving the men to glare after her.

She came to Wilhelmina and smiled broadly. "Come inside. Let's have tea." Gladys gave Marcus a pointed look. "You will let her spend a few minutes visiting, won't you?"

Marcus didn't dare look at her. "Yes, of course. Tobias and I need to pick up medication from Evan and load up the wagon."

Marcus then addressed his wife. "I'll be by for you in an hour or so," he told her and walked off.

The women settled in the back of the mercantile where Gemina goaded her husband to bring chairs for them. Tea was made and a pretty plate of cookies was passed. Wilhelmina was delighted to spend time with the women and almost cried with joy when Isabel burst into the store calling out her name before hugging her tightly.

The day went by much too fast. After tea, the women all assisted with shopping for the winter. Gemina gave her almost as much as she purchased, insisting it was a wedding gift.

"If only you lived closer," Isabel said with a woeful look. "I could help sew dresses."

When Marcus and Tobias returned, the women lined up to hug Wilhelmina and Eleanor. Finally, they were bustled into the wagon to head home.

It was good to see his wife so happy. She and Eleanor held an animated conversation the entire ride back. They recounted every single conversation of the time with the other ladies. Seeing the sparkle in her eyes and her wide smile lightened his heart. Once spring came, he'd see to it that she traveled to town often to visit with her new friends.

They arrived home a short time later and, after everything was unloaded, Marcus helped Wilhelmina out of her coat. He pressed a kiss to her soft cheek and she let out a sigh.

"I hope you're in a better mood and not so mad at me."

She turned to him with a brow lifted. "I am in a wonderful mood. However, I am still not happy with you. We..." she motioned between them. "Still have a discussion pending."

"How many times do I have to explain there is nothing to dis..."

"There is much to discuss..." she gritted out and her nostrils flared. "I am not sure what to say to you...I need to walk away." Not waiting for his reply, she darted out of his reach and walked to the back of the house.

Marcus walked outside scratching his head. He had to admit his wife had spunk. The fire in her beautiful whiskey-brown eyes had almost made him smile. Now she was angry once again. He looked to the house and wondered what she was doing at the moment.

It made no sense. Why would she want to talk about

something when it wouldn't change? Women were interesting, but admittedly, very hard to figure out.

When his father came out and sat down on the porch with a pipe, Marcus walked over. "Hey, Pa. You see Wilhelmina?"

"Caught a sight of her dashing through the house as if her skirts were on fire. What'd you do now?"

Although it was cold, he was not ready to go inside. Since boyhood, he'd always preferred the outdoors, often having to be called in for supper. More times than he could count, he'd missed it altogether. He'd often begged for permission to sleep outside where he could stare at the skies for hours. It had been a long time since he'd done that.

"I told her it was no use in talking about something when a decision is made. Not sure why she's so mad."

"What decision is this?" His father lit the pipe and waited for his reply.

It was a hard subject to speak about out loud, especially with his father. "I decided we'd remain here through the winter. I want to be available in case something's needed for Mother."

"What does Wilhelmina think about it?"

He frowned. "What do you mean?"

"Does she agree? Would she prefer to move into the house you built and visit regularly? What is her preference on the matter?"

"I don't know. All she says is that I didn't discuss it before making the decision."

His father's steady gaze met his. "I suggest you find out how she feels about it. Son, it doesn't matter whether you're right or wrong when it comes to marriage. What matters is that you know how your wife feels."

The words resonated and he lowered to sit. Looking back, he remembered many times his parents had obviously argued and were mad at each other. His mother's stoic face and his father's avoidance of looking at her made a tangible air of discomfort in their presence. Each time, he'd often wondered why they'd disagreed.

Usually a day or two later, things between his parents were smoothed out and back to normal. He didn't like it when they were mad at each other.

"I suppose I'll talk to her. But she's pretty angry."

His father's chuckle drifted across the porch. "She's a feisty one, that's for sure. Perfect match for you if you ask me. You'll have to do more than talk at this point. Especially if you hurt her feelings."

Hurting Wilhelmina was the one thing he didn't want to do. If he'd hurt her in any way, he'd feel horrible. "You think I did?"

"There's only one way to find out, Son."

He walked inside and headed for the bedroom.

She stood by the wardrobe, one hand on a dress, her expression soft. It was easy to tell, in her mind, she was elsewhere, probably back in the comfort of her home, a familiar place.

No matter what circumstances had taken her so far away, he admired the courage within her that she'd take such a chance and follow her heart to an unfamiliar territory. Here in Montana, she was virtually without friends or relatives of any sort. Only her wits to call her own and whatever she carried with her, were the only familiar items linking her to where she'd come from.

She turned to look at him and his heart lurched at the shiny telltale sign of unshed tears. Wilhelmina was an astonishingly beautiful woman, even when angry. He could not fathom why she'd had to travel out west to marry.

"Is something the matter?" She asked him the question he should be asking her. "You seem troubled."

With a defiant lift of her chin, Marcus recognized it was not a question of concern, but more a goading, indicating she thought he would not ask the same. "I came to talk. You are upset and I aim to find out why."

For a split second, her eyes widened and he expected

her to strike back at him. Instead, she shook her head and went to a chair, putting more distance between them. Hands folded on her lap, she looked up at him. "I am upset for several reasons. The first being that you do not seem to listen to what I say."

He bristled at the words but, remembering he'd come prepared to hear her out, he sat down on the bed. "I'm listening now."

"Very well. It is not that I object to remaining here through the winter. Nor do I blame you for wanting to stay." She seemed to struggle with how to continue, but at his silence she did. "You hurt my feelings. It is as if my opinion doesn't count. That I have no say."

"You matter very much." Marcus considered her words, still not quite understanding fully. "I will do my best to discuss things with you in the future."

"Thank you. That is all I ask."

She stood and removed her robe, folded it and placed it neatly over the back of the chair.

The silence in the room once she climbed into bed made Marcus uncomfortable. By the thickness in the air, something else hung in the balance. An idea that, perhaps, she needed reassurance struck and he climbed into bed and pulled her into his arms.

"I'm sorry." Marcus pressed a kiss to her temple, immediately gratified when she sighed and relaxed into him.

One kiss led to another until they made love, learning each other and becoming one with the expectation of what would come next.


"Good morning," Wilhelmina said to her sister-in-law. Eleanor stopped short in the doorway of the kitchen. "Breakfast is almost complete."

Eleanor smiled broadly, looking at the filled platters. "What a nice surprise."

It had been two weeks since Wilhelmina and Marcus had made up. And every day she'd learned more and more from Eleanor.

In a way, remaining there was a blessing. When spring finally came, she'd feel more comfortable running a home on her own.

There were still things she'd not do. The scrubbing of floors, for instance, on her hands and knees was something she'd already asked the woman who came about doing and they'd come to an agreement.

Eleanor moved closer, a frown replacing her previous smile. "Mother is not well. She had a bad night."

"Is the doctor coming?"

"Pa is not sure he wants to send for him just yet."

Around the table, there were tight lines around mouths and stilted conversation. Wilhelmina had spent the day before reading to Elaine who was too weak to hold up the book and finish it. Although the woman was ill, her quick wit and comments had them both laughing. Death was never fair and this family would soon weather the storm of it.

"I won't be working today," Jacob Hamilton said, not looking at anyone in particular. "Need to see about bringing the youngest of the herd closer to shelter and finish the addition to the stables. Tobias, you and Owen need to scout for any lost cattle. It's going to be a cold one, don't need any stranded critters."

The patriarch looked to Marcus. "Go to town. Ask if Doctor Jones can come see about your mother."

Once breakfast was done, everyone but Marcus left the room. His gaze met hers. "Do you need anything from town?"

"No, thank you," Wilhelmina stood and wrapped her arms around his waist. There was no way to make what he faced easier. All she could do was be there for him and offer comfort.

His strong arms wrapped around Wilhelmina as his

chest expanded with a long breath. She closed her eyes, her face against his breast.

"I'll be back in a few hours." His voice was gruff with emotion.

He didn't return that day, or the next.

The worst days brought out Wilhelmina's determination. She handled the reins of the horse as she and Eleanor rode toward town for the second time that day, stopping along each homestead and asking about Marcus.

Exhausted with grief and worry, neither of them spoke much to each other. Both of them were too tired of speculating what could have happened.

The only person left at the house was Jacob, who looked over his sick wife and strove to keep her in the dark about what happened.

The distance between the Hamilton ranch and Laurel was not long, perhaps two hours at the most now that it was snowing. There was little danger as a heavily traveled road was easy to traverse.

Whatever had happened to Marcus either had to do with an accident or with an occurrence in town.

When they arrived in Laurel, Eleanor took over and guided the horse to a post before climbing down. "There's James." She motioned across the street. Her husband stood speaking with Howard Johnston, the mercantile owner, who pointed toward a building.

Wilhelmina turned to where the man pointed. It was the saloon.

"If he's been in there this entire time..."

Eleanor shook her head with fervor. "He would never do anything when our mother's health is so bad. Perhaps someone in there saw him."

They climbed down from the wagon just as James

neared. "Howard overheard someone in the saloon talking about a horse coming into town without a rider. I'm going in to find the man. Can you two check at the local stable and see if it's Marcus' horse?"

The horse was his. Wilhelmina's legs wobbled upon Eleanor's proclaiming it to be. Something terrible happened to Marcus and while he lay somewhere hurt, she'd thought the worst of him.

The stable handler, a burly, bearded man scratched at his face with a grubby hand. "The horse came from the west side of town. I suggest you go back that way and search."

"Oh my goodness, why didn't we think of that? Of course, it's a shorter route. It's a bit harder to traverse. But knowing Marcus, he tried to take a short cut."

"We should go search now." Wilhelmina could not help a tear that trickled down her face. "It's so cold at night. He must be freezing."

"It's too late. We won't be able to see a thing." James had walked up, his face grim. "If he's out there, at least he was wearing a warm coat."

Wilhelmina gritted her teeth. "I'll go alone then."

"You can't. It's bad enough traveling that road during daylight. It's too rocky and unsteady."

"I'll put the horses up," James interjected. "Go to the boarding house and get a room. We'll leave a first daylight."

Wilhelmina looked up at the darkening sky and said a prayer that Marcus be able to sustain one more night alone.

Marcus shivered, no longer able to control the constant shaking. He couldn't stand or sit. The pain that thundered up from his broken leg had already caused him to pass out twice. Instead, he moaned and clenched his jaw as inch by inch, he'd dragged himself to where, hopefully, someone would spot him.

It had been so foolish to travel this way. Unused, the overgrown trail made a perfect place for critters to hide. There were holes in the ground and uneven shifting rocks.

A critter had spooked his horse, causing it to buck, sending Marcus to the ground. Then his foot had caught on the stirrup and the damned horse dragged him for a bit before he'd finally been able to get free. From what he could tell, he'd broken his hip and ankle as well as his leg.

He reached for a long branch and placed it over his lap. Even if he managed to splint the leg, there was no way to stand with a broken hipbone.

With only one portion of the branch fastened, Marcus was sweating from the exertion. Trembling, he fell back, immediately regretting the movement as his hip throbbed and, once again, unable to withstand the pain and weak from lack of food or water, darkness claimed him.

The sun was still up when he finally came to. "Help," he called out, but his voice cracked and was softer than he hoped. Three days now, by his calculation as the sun was almost setting, yet again. Although the nights were bitterly cold, it helped soothe the pain somewhat. Unfortunately, the raging fever caused sweating, so his shirt was drenched. It was impossible to prepare for what the night would bring and a part of him wished not to wake up the next morning.

Once the starkness of morning came, he'd have to make it through another day. He knew it was most probable he'd not survive much longer.

A picture of Wilhelmina formed. His wife had brightened the last weeks. Interesting how, up until then, he'd not considered life with a woman and now he grieved the loss.

As the day continued and he faced possible death, Marcus considered how if things were switched, he could not fathom life without her. A smile curved his lips at the thought. Every day, he hurried home after working because she'd be there in the house.

Every evening, once supper ended, he could hardly wait for bedtime and the opportunity to be alone with the beauty. She'd proven to be most knowledgeable, their conversations often going until late in the night. Of course, making love with her still awed him. She was passionate and eager to please him.

Now, she'd be a widow. He wondered who she would marry. No doubt it would happen. A woman so attractive would not suffer for suitors. The thought angered him and Marcus adjusted, only to scream in pain.

A sound permeated through his foggy senses, someone came. Voices called out his name and he lifted an arm. "Here!" Unfortunately his voice was but a hoarse whisper.

Marcus was so weak it took all his energy to lift a thin branch and wave it. His arm, too heavy to maintain up, plopped beside him and he let out a curse. It sounded like his brother-in-law, James. The voice called again, this time nearer.

It was move, or die there alone. Marcus turned to his healthy hip and pushed up. He shook from the exertion and cried out as his body disobeyed his command and he collapsed.


"Over here!" James called out. Wilhelmina climbed down from the wagon and ran toward where James stood.

She searched the ground until noticing the figure of someone in the dirt. "Marcus!" She pushed James aside to rush to his side. With a gasp, she lifted her husband's head. He was unconscious, but alive. "Oh my God. He's burning up with fever. We must get him to town immediately."

James crouched down and touched her shoulder. "His leg looks to be broken. Good thing he's out because this would otherwise hurt pretty bad." He stood. "Stay here, I'll figure out how to bring the wagon a bit closer." James took his jacket off and placed it over Marcus.

His face was purpled and bruised, skin was torn from his knuckles and his coat was torn to shreds. From what she could figure, the horse had dragged him. She looked down his body noticing he'd splinted his left foot. "Oh no, Marcus. How you must have suffered." She kissed his heated forehead and held him against her.

Eleanor approached, her face wet with tears. "I was too afraid to come closer until James told me he's alive." She collapsed next to Marcus and lifted his hand, kissing it and holding it to her face. "Marcus?"

He didn't stir, but it was probably for the best at the moment. Eleanor searched his face. "He has a fever?"

"Yes, he does and from the looks of it, broke his left leg. Probably why he had no choice but to stay here."

The sound of boots crunching over the ground was followed by James' stern voice. "You two pick him up under the arms, I'll take his legs. If he comes to, he may struggle. Don't let go."

They had quite a time getting Marcus into the back of the wagon. Thankfully, James had spread blankets on the floorboard, which would make unloading him easier. The solemn man looked to them. "Stay back here with him and try to keep him steady. Unfortunately, this trail is uneven. It will be a bumpy ride."

Marcus moaned and both immediately soothed him. The ride to Laurel seemed to take an eternity. Wilhelmina continually searched his face for any signs of awakening, but other than several moans when the wagon bumped, he remained in an unconscious state.

By the time they returned to town, Tobias was there along with two men who assisted in unloading Marcus at the clinic. Wilhelmina wringed her hands for the few moments she was away from him and then rushed to his side once he was settled atop a narrow bed.

Evan Jones acknowledged her with a slight lift of his jaw. Seeming to gather it was fruitless to do so, he did not ask her to leave.

"I'm going to cut off his boot. It's good he did not remove it, the break would have caused swelling. Unfortunately, it may have cut off circulation which could be bad."

Once the boot was removed, with the help of the doctor's nurse and Wilhelmina, they removed Marcus' other clothing.

His lower back was scratched badly, as were his hands. Other than minor bruising elsewhere, the main concern was his left leg. The area was an ugly mixture of dark purple bruising and yellowing. His left ankle was swollen to twice the size of his right, but the doctor pronounced it would heal.

"His hip is misplaced, must have hurt mighty bad," the doctor informed her. "If he comes to, he'll pass back out when we try to pop it back in."

The doctor prodded Marcus' upper leg. "Another fracture." The doctor shook his head, his brows drawn. With each pronunciation and mumble, Wilhelmina held back the urge to cry.

"He'll recover." Evan finally finished his examination and then gave her a distracted look as if he'd forgotten she was there. "Wilhelmina, please get Tobias and James. They'll have to help. I suggest you step outside."

She clung to Eleanor moments later when Marcus' screams echoed through the rooms. "He must have come to," Eleanor stated the obvious. "The pain must have woken him."

The next scream tore through Wilhelmina and her eyes widened. "I should be there."

"No, let's wait. We'd only get in the way."

The doctor's nurse walked from another room, her warm gaze falling on them. "I brought some valerian root tea for your nerves. The doctor will have to splint and wrap the leg. Afterwards, Marcus will be sedated. Once that is done, you can see him."

They drank the tea in silence. Each time a sound came from the other room, both Wilhelmina and Eleanor would jump. The tea helped, although it felt frivolous to be drinking tea at a time such as this.

Wilhelmina prayed in silence. Marcus would have a long recovery, at least until spring. Somehow, she'd manage taking care of him and helping Eleanor with everything else. All that mattered was that her husband was found alive and would return home with her.

Home.

She took a shaky breath and looked to Eleanor. Her sister-in-law reached over and squeezed her hand. "Everything will be fine."

Wilhelmina nodded. "Yes, it will."

A breath caught in her throat and she sighed.

For the first time in her life, she was in love. In love with Marcus Hamilton.

A soft smile curved her lips as tears flowed down her face.

# Chapter Thirteen

Winter hit Laurel, Montana full force bringing bitter wind and heavy snowfall. Every day, the men would excavate a path to the stable and barn to see about the livestock. The heavier workload, since Marcus was unable to help, had them exhausted and grumpy in the evenings.

Even the women seemed affected as they maintained stern, solemn expressions as each dreary day passed. Through the window, there were gray skies and snow as far as the eye could see.

Marcus' mood was no exception. He grew tired of remaining bedbound for weeks followed by sitting indoors while the others, his father included, did all the work. He'd never been one to shirk away from hard work and believed in doing his fair share. However, barely able to walk, he would be more of a hindrance.

After pulling crutches under his arms, he rose to stand and hobbled to the front door. Surely, there was something he could do to help.

"You'll only get in the way and create more work for them when you fall on your behind and have to be dragged back inside." Wilhelmina looked up from her sewing. "If you need something to do, help Eleanor with the peas or paint the table you made."

"I can't paint outside, it's too cold," he grumbled and hobbled toward the kitchen. How the woman could read his mind still amazed him. Without complaint, she'd nursed him through some pretty embarrassing moments while he recovered. She had taken care of his every basic need with barely a sign of annoyance. True, several times his temper had made him snap at her, but she'd given it right back to him.

"I'll go lie down for a bit."

"No, you won't."

He slid a look at her. "Why not?"

"Because you need to move around. Could you please go check on your mother for me? I will go make tea and warm up some soup for her."

His parents' bedroom had been aired out. The curtains were moved aside to allow for what little sunshine there was to come through. Atop a small table by the bed was a glass vase with sprigs of evergreen, bringing the scent of the outdoors inside the room.

His mother looked to him when he entered and her lips curved. "I'm so glad to see you moving about. You gave us quite a scare." The weakness in her voice made his chest tighten. "Come here, sweetheart, sit by me."

He did as she bid, lowering to a chair where his father usually sat. Marcus took her hand between his. "How are you today, Ma?"

"I wish I could say better." Her reply was accompanied by a wince. "I don't know how much longer I can hang on."

"Don't say that," he told her, willing her to look at him with reassurance.

"Promise me, you'll be happy."

"Ma."

"Listen, please," she said with a pleading look. "I need you to promise me you'll see about Tobias getting settled, too."

"I promise." It was best to agree and not get her upset, he decided. Listening to her words made it clear how badly she felt.

"There's something else. Your father. He is still young." She faltered, the last word catching in her throat. "I want him to remarry. Once all of you move out, he'll be here by himself. I've already spoken to Eleanor about this. I want him to marry again and find happiness. I love him too much to think he'll spend the rest of his years alone."

Her eyes shined with unshed tears and his heart tore to pieces. "Ma, I don't think he'll be willing to do that."

"I know he'll balk. That's why you, your brother and sister will be there to help him through."

"What if it were Pa? Do you think he'd want you to marry?"

Her chuckle was weak. "I'm not sure, but I probably would anyway."

The familiar mischievous twinkle in her eyes made him smile in return. "You would."

Her hand stirred and she squeezed his, lines around her mouth tightening with pain. "Give me some laudanum. I can't take this pain without it."

"Wilhelmina is bringing tea. I'll tell her to put some drops into it."

"Thank you." Her gaze met his and he could see only love. How lucky he'd been to be raised by a woman like her, someone who'd always been there for him and his siblings. Never for an instant did he doubt she loved him with the strength of a mother bear, defending and protecting her children, always nurturing.

His father would be lost without her if she were to go. Jacob Hamilton, although headstrong and unbending to most, drew his strength from his wife.

There was no doubt in Marcus' mind that his marriage to Wilhelmina would be like that. Both of them drawing strength from the other.

A ray of sunshine broke through the clouds, lighting up

the room. His mother's lips curved and she stretched her hand up to it. "Thank you."

Her head lulled to the side and she let out one last breath.


The tray in Wilhelmina's hands slipped to the floor, the crash of dishes dulled by the lurch of her heart.

Elaine's head lay to the side, her lifeless eyes staring straight ahead to the window.

Marcus sat in the chair next to the bed, his upper body draped across his mother. The wide shoulders shuddered as he cried.

"Eleanor!" she called out. "Come."

Instead of going to Marcus, she stood aside to allow his sister to enter. Eleanor gasped and put her fist up to her mouth, barely stifling the long cry. "Oh no. Mama?" She rushed to the bed and curved her hands on her mother's face. "No."

Marcus did not look up, but remained in place. His face was hidden in the folds of the blankets and his mother's nightshift.

"I'll go find the others." Wilhelmina stooped to pick up the broken cup and bowl, quickly mopping up what she could with the napkin.


Wilhelmina shook from more than the cold knowing she'd bring dreaded news to the men who now stood over a bonfire warming their hands.

As it turned out, she did not have to utter a word. Jacob took one look at her face and broke out in a run towards the house, Tobias and James on his heels.

Instead of returning to the house, she neared the fire. The warmth of the flames fanned over her wet face. It was then she realized why the men had not needed her to say anything.

The silence of the surroundings brought her peace and she inhaled deeply, not wanting to move. Elaine Hamilton was no longer in pain, but everyone in the house would be torn apart by grief and would hurt for many days. It would be a hard, bitter winter in more ways than she'd ever expected.

*Philadelphia, Pennsylvania*

Aurora Middleton reread Wilhelmina's letter, a sense of pride in her friend's courage filling her. After turning Wilhelmina down when she'd suggested they move in together and live independently, for many nights she'd tossed in bed wishing to be brave enough to do such a thing.

Her future was in a tight grasp of responsibility. She spent her days lonely and alone, not leaving her room to even consider doing anything that polite society considered unacceptable. The grim view from her window offering leafless trees, cloudy, gray skies and misting, mirrored her feelings.

Lucille, her maid and only friend now, came to the doorway. "Gilda Wilkins and her mother have arrived."

Aurora held back a groan. Since Wilhelmina's departure, the two had been insistent on building a friendship. Of course, it was a ploy to get into the Jamesons' inner circle. Her upcoming marriage to the eldest would cement Aurora a lofty position in local society, which translated to constant visitors and many attempts at new friendships.

"Show them in please, Lucille, and bring tea. Thank you," she said to her friend with a smile.

Lucille neared. "I can tell them you're unwell."

"I appreciate it," Aurora replied and squeezed Lucille's

hand. "But I better go see what they want. It won't be a long visit."

She almost giggled when Lucille gave her a wide-eyed look. "Right."

Before standing to greet her visitors, she folded Wilhelmina's letter and placed it in her pocket. She'd replied as soon as she'd gotten it, hoping her friend would receive it before the weather precluded mail delivery.

Gilda and her mother, Laverne, glided in with pasted on smiles and ready hugs of greeting. Once seated, both scanned over her attire, as if memorizing it for future reference of some sort.

"Lucille is bringing tea," Aurora told them by way of greeting, unsure what they'd concoct as a reason for their early afternoon visit.

"I am so glad that you were free for company. This dreadful weather makes for dull days indoors, wouldn't you say?" It was Laverne, the mother, who started the conversation with not quite a lively subject. The weather, of course, was a safe place to start, although not much more entertaining than her view through the window.

"Yes, I agree. Quite dull."

"I love your dress," Gilda piped up. "Did you have it made here locally?"

She'd visited Wilhelmina many times wearing the dress, but she refrained from commenting about it. Instead, she nodded. "I did. Wilhelmina and I always used the same seamstress. She has one identical, only a different fabric."

On mentioning her friend's name, both stiffened and glanced at each other. Finally, Laverne spoke. "Have you heard from her? I am horribly worried."

If it were true, they would have asked two visits earlier. Aurora nodded. "Yes, I have. Oh, there's Lucille now. Should we adjourn to the table, ladies?"

Thankfully, she was able to claim an appointment and the women were dispatched as soon as they finished tea over awkward attempts to gain an invitation to the Jamesons' winter party.

Aurora sat back and closed her eyes.

"Aurora, did you forget we are going to the Jamesons for tea?" Her mother waltzed in already dressed in a deep purple gown that flattered her fair skin. "Get dressed. The coach will be ready shortly."

A shudder at knowing she'd spend several hours at her fiancé's house ran over her. "Is that today?" Her futile attempt in hopes her mother was wrong was quickly stopped by a sharp look.

"I'll be only a few moments." She rushed from the room.

In her bedroom, as she removed her dress, Wilhelmina's letter brushed against her fingers.

Why did she continually read it? Was it because she faced a life tied to a domineering man who'd not minced words letting her know he expected to rule over her body, soul and mind? Milford Jameson had been groomed to take over the family's dynasty. He was indulged and pampered, which resulted in an entitled ass in Aurora's opinion.

She glanced at the letter once more before placing it into her writing box. Then she turned to her bed where a dressed had already been laid out for her. It seemed that from now on, little was left in the way of choices.

# Chapter Fourteen

Marcus took a tentative step without the crutches. Since his mother's death, he could barely stand the indoors. Even more, he hated being confined to using crutches to bear his weight.

On his right, Wilhelmina rushed to him with arms extended, as if to catch him in case he fell. Eleanor watched from the kitchen doorway, an ever-present scowl marring her pretty face.

"Be careful," Wilhelmina said, moving closer.

"I'm not a damned child," Marcus snapped. He instantly regretted it when Wilhelmina straightened, her eyes rounded.

Eleanor let out a grunt. "You are such a bear these days. She's only trying to encourage you and all you do is bite at her. If you fall, neither of us will help you up."

Wilhelmina turned away, but not before he saw hurt in her expression. Winter was always difficult. Being indoors for hours on end, and with the added burden of grief, it made everyone on edge.

"I'm sorry," he said, turning to her. There was little discomfort today. His ankle was still tender and would remain braced but, thankfully, his hip held him up without much more than a slight twinge. His leg had healed quicker than expected.

When she turned, her gaze met his evenly. "You apologize daily. It concerns me that you consider it acceptable to be annoyed and say things that hurt me because you consider that an apology will suffice to settle things."

"I don't like being treated as if I'm an invalid and can't do for myself."

"And for many days, you could not. I care enough to worry you'll hurt yourself, but I see you prefer I don't. Have it your way. I won't care from now on." Her skirts brushed his leg as she rounded him and headed to the back of the house.

His brother came up and nudged him. "Wanna come to the barn and help me clean out stalls?"

"Yeah. I'll try." He limped to get his coat and hat. Then he walked outside with Tobias who frowned up at the sky.

His brother shook his head. "How much longer before we can get Pa to leave the bedroom for more than supper. I understand he's grieving, but I'm worried about him. He's drawn, lost a lot of weight."

It was then Marcus realized he'd been so focused on his own situation he'd not paid much attention to their father. "I don't know."

"The weather isn't as bad this week. Perhaps, Pastor Ward and his daughter can come for a visit." Tobias pulled his coat collar up.

"Are you sweet on Isabel Ward?" It occurred to Marcus it had been a while since he and his brother spoke. It was nice to do so, felt normal. "She's a pretty little thing."

"Nah." Tobias shrugged. "I am not. She's a bit young and, besides, Ma and Eleanor placed the ad."

They arrived at the barn and the animals bellowed in response, knowing they'd be fed. Despite the chill outside, it was comfortable in the barn and they began working. Marcus was slow, but the work gave him an outlet for his inner turmoil.

"Maybe I'll get lucky and get a wife like Wilhelmina. She sure is a good woman. Pretty, too."

Marcus grunted in reply. "Good luck. I doubt there's another one as beautiful as my wife."

Tobias was silent. Marcus turned to find his brother had come over to where he was working. "What is it?"

It was comical to see the wide grin split Tobias' face. "You are in love."

"What if I am?" he snapped and continued working. "Why is it so funny?"

"Now I know why you've been a bear to live with. You're scared she doesn't feel the same way." Tobias roared with laughter. "It would suit you right."

"You need to get back to work."

"And you need to admit you're scared."

Before he could reply, James arrived at the barn. The stern man grumbled about the cold, grabbed a pitchfork and climbed the ladder to the hayloft.

"What's got you?" Tobias said looking up.

"Eleanor just kicked me out of the house. Said I was being difficult." James pitched a large bale over the side with so much force it bounced. "Damned if that woman doesn't drive me to drink."

Once again, Tobias began to laugh. "I might be the lucky one, not to have to worry about what my wife does or doesn't do. You two are enough to convince a man to remain single."

Laughter ceased when the second bale barely missed Tobias. "Hey, watch out." His brother glowered up at the loft. "You almost got me."

"My aim must be off," James replied.

If Marcus didn't change his attitude, Wilhelmina wasn't sure what she'd do. Today, she'd come close to screaming at him. After raising her voice twice already that week, it would not do. Of course, everyone was tired of the seclusion. She understood that but, at the same time, it didn't give him permission to be rude.

She looked around their bedroom. Everything was in its place, the clothes either hanging or neatly folded. Every sock and undergarment laundered. She'd finished knitting a sweater for Marcus and was now making him a scarf. The yarn and needles were in a basket by the window beside a pair of chairs Marcus had made.

Tobias and James planned to go to town the following day and she was anxious, hoping Aurora had written back. It would be nice to hear back from her dear friend and receive news about home and her father. She could care less about Gilda and Laverne, both more of a thorn from the past than anything else.

Perhaps spending time outdoors would help Marcus' mood. She, for one, had enough and would not put up with it. Tonight, she'd speak to him and try to get through to the man how hurtful his words could be at times.

Although she doubted it would do much good.


That night, the candlelight flickered over the bedroom as Wilhelmina lay next to Marcus on the bed. He looked up at the ceiling in thought. "I understand what you said. It's just that I was trying to make a point not to hover over me when I was trying to walk."

"You could have said it in a nicer way, not by cursing."

He was silent for a few moments and Wilhelmina wanted to elbow him in the ribs. The man would put a mule to shame. Stubborn as the day was long.

"I apologized. I should not have cussed." He rolled to face her and scanned her face. The man was too handsome for his own good. With long lashes and straight eyebrows, it always looked as if he flirted. His lips thinned for a moment. "I love you."

Wilhelmina knew her eyes became wide as saucers at the unexpected declaration. "What?"

"I don't know when it happened. I love you." Marcus didn't seem too pleased at his pronouncement, which made Wilhelmina want to laugh.

"I would think that if you do, you'd strive to be nicer to me," she replied, touching the tip of his nose.

He looked away for a moment. "I'm not sure what is going on." Closing the distance between them, he pressed his lips to hers. "I miss being with you. This injury and all."

They'd not made love since the accident, having tried once without success as Marcus hurt too badly to continue.

"Do you want to try? We can take it slowly." Wilhelmina's heart quickened when he reached for her.

Their mouths met with a mixture of trepidation and hunger. She clung to him. Her need for him took over any other emotion.

Lovemaking was tender, sweet and slow. Every sensation took the forefront, from longing to exhilaration, until she floated away on a cloud of so many emotions Wilhelmina could only cry out.

The weight of Marcus over her was just right as he, too, let go and fell into the abyss. His hoarse voice sounded wonderful in her ear.

"I love you, too, Marcus."

Marcus lifted his head, his gaze boring into hers. "Do you really?"

"For a long time now. It's probably the only reason I have not smothered you to death while you slept."

He laughed. "I'll remember to be nicer to you in the future if you've had those thoughts."

It was nice to relax with him, to once again be able to talk and relax with each other. Wilhelmina hoped it was a new start and that a new, better chapter in their marriage was reached.

His palm cupped her face, lifting it up to his. "I will do my best to listen, be more attentive and..." His brow creased as he tried to figure out what else to say.

Wilhelmina pressed a kissed on Marcus' mouth. "Reasonable?"

"Yes, that."

"Goodnight," she said, giving him a sleepy kiss.

Her response was a soft snore.

The next morning, Wilhelmina stretched. She gasped when she realized Marcus remained in bed. Usually, he woke hours before she did, if only to annoy Eleanor in the kitchen. He slept soundly, his face turned toward her. Lips parted and a lock of hair across his cheek, Marcus looked years younger. The crinkle between his brows, the ever-present, attractive scowl, was replaced with smooth skin.

Although cranky at times, she had to admit her husband was more willing to listen to her now. Although he'd balked at her for attempting to assist him, he'd always thanked her for whatever chores she did and complimented her attempts to cook and such. Although her culinary skills still required a lot of honing, she never felt as if her efforts were in vain.

As a matter of fact, Tobias and Jacob were both the same way. Complimentary and thankful to both her and Eleanor for everything they did. From what she knew, most men took women's work for granted, not seeming to appreciate the hard work. Especially there in the west where women were responsible for every aspect from churning the butter to pumping water for meals and cleaning. One would hope men would be more appreciative.

Marcus inhaled and opened his eyes. "Good morning." His lips curved and he lifted a brow.

Her smile turned to shock when her husband pulled her against him and began nuzzling her neck.

"Oh."

Once the men ate breakfast, they all went out doors. Tobias

and James would be hitching a large sleigh to plow horses and heading to town, while Marcus planned to check on the animals.

"Pa, can you come with me? I'm still not too steady."

Jacob jerked up from studying his coffee. "I will, yes. Let me get a thicker shirt on."

Marcus and Tobias shared a look, which told Wilhelmina they hoped to get their father interested in more than remaining locked up. It was time for him to do more than mourn.

Admittedly, her own father had grieved for over a year before he'd been willing to leave their house and to accompany her to social events. The long months had served to strengthen him but, at the same time, he'd been easy prey for Laverne. She was the first woman her father escorted out after becoming a widower.

Eleanor fussed over James, reminding him to travel with care. She wrapped a scarf about his neck and followed by doing the same to Tobias. "Don't take the short cut. If it gets late, stay the night and wait for the morning to come back."

"It only takes a couple hours to get there," James grumbled. But by the soft smile, he didn't mind his wife fussing over him. "Don't worry." He kissed her temple.

"See you at supper time." Tobias escaped before Eleanor could turn back to him, rushing out the door holding the lists both she and Eleanor had made for them.

Eleanor and Wilhelmina went out to the porch and watched them ride away. "Finally, a quiet time in the house. I love James and my brothers, but boy are they a nuisance to have around during the day."

Wilhelmina chuckled. "Right you are. How about we air out the house a bit? I'll sweep the front rooms."

"And I'll scrub that dining table and kitchen counters. All the soot from the stove has gotten into everything."

Wilhelmina looked to Eleanor. "Once spring comes, what are we going to do? I'm going to miss you."

"I hadn't thought much about it. But you're right. James and I have decided to stay here. I can't see leaving Pa alone with Tobias. Neither of them can cook more than beans."

"We can take turns," Wilhelmina offered.

"No," Eleanor reached for her arm and patted her. "You're a newlywed. You need to start your married life alone with your husband."

Eleanor saw the look of concern on Wilhelmina's face. "James and I have been married for almost six years now. We've only lived here a year. I don't mind. It's like my own home now. Once Tobias marries, if he ever does, then I'll move to the other house."

The thought of living with her husband alone made Wilhelmina even more impatient for spring to arrive. Not only would the weather warm, but also there was so much to look forward to.

She turned to the doorway and lost her balance. Everything swam before her and she rushed to the end of the porch to throw up.

"That was quick," Eleanor said laughing. "You and Marcus did not waste any time."

The spell was over as fast as it came. Wilhelmina straightened. "Something must have not sat well."

"Either that or I can expect a niece or nephew by fall."

When everything tilted this time, she leaned on the wall and Eleanor came to her. "Perhaps, you need to rest just for a bit before tackling those floors."

Wilhelmina allowed her sister-in-law to hold her elbow as they walked inside.

"I wonder what Marcus will say when he finds out," Eleanor said.

Wilhelmina shook her head. "Not yet. Let's wait to be sure."

# Chapter Fifteen

It felt good to be mobile again. Marcus continued brushing his horse while the contented animal ate fresh oats. Although winter had definitely set in, he didn't mind it as much as he normally would. Funny how certain things could change a man's perspective.

Tobias grunted, stretching. "Some days I wonder if it's all worth it, you know?"

Not sure where the conversation was going, Marcus nodded. "Yep."

"Pa has had it all; land, a good wife, us. Then one day, none of it matters. I don't think I want to go through all that."

"What are you saying?" Marcus went to the edge of the stall to get a good look at Tobias' expression.

Head bent, overly long hair curtained his face. "I mean. Why put myself through it? In the end, we're all going to end up planted out there."

It was strange to see his normally easygoing brother so morose. Come to think of it, Tobias had been different since their mother died. Introspective and quiet, he'd gone through the motions that were required during the day. The after supper, he went to his bedroom, not to emerge until morning.

Even though younger than him, Tobias was taller and broader. And although Tobias was the more passive of the two, his brother didn't shirk from a fistfight whenever Marcus instigated trouble.

"That's life, Brother. Have to take what we can, make the best out of it while we can. You'll see."

His brother's bright green eyes met his. "That's just it. I don't think I want to. If someone answers that ad Eleanor posted, I'm not writing back." Tobias raked his fingers through his hair, yanking them past knots and cussing. "Need a damned haircut."

"I'm surprised Eleanor hasn't caught you," Marcus said with a chuckle. "She'd normally cut it by now."

With a scowl, Tobias grabbed a handful. "Before long, I'll have to pin it up." He lifted his hair and spoke in a high voice. "Let me see about supper. Don't you boys come sniffin' around either." He imitated Eleanor perfectly and both laughed.

After Tobias went back to his chores, Marcus looked after his younger brother. He'd have to talk to Wilhelmina about the conversation. Perhaps she'd have some insight. He'd promised their mother that he'd make sure Tobias was happy.

What he didn't expect was for this change in him.

*My Dearest Wilhelmina,*

*I hope this letter arrives before winter's end and that it finds you well. It is impossible to put into words how much I miss you.*

*Your letter is becoming worn from the many times I have reread it. By the time you read this, I'm sure to have read it several times more.*

*The horrible reality of how my life will turn out becomes more and more apparent with each social engagement and time I have to spend with the Jamesons.*

*If only I could be as brave as you. A more courageous*

*woman I have yet to meet. That you took a chance to find your own way amazes me daily.*

*Your stepsister and stepmother have visited me regularly. As you can guess, it's quite apparent their attempts at friendship have nothing to do with me personally, but my new status in society.*

*At times, I find their attempts to find something remotely familiar to speak about while at the same time avoiding mentioning you quite entertaining. I often bring you up just to get a reaction. Is that terrible of me? How can they not miss you as much as I do?*

*Preparations for the wedding have started. Mostly my mother and Lady Jameson, who seem to act as if they are going to be the bride. My input, when it is requested, is quickly discarded. Which to be honest does not bother me in the least.*

*I have gone so far as to imagine Milford marring my mother, so then I could go on with my life. — Yes, I'm laughing.*

*As much as I dreamed of my wedding day, I find myself dreading it more each passing moment.*

*If only I could meet that handsome husband of yours. I'd congratulate him on finding such a treasure in a wife.*

*Please write me again soon.*

*With fond wishes for a wonderful life, your friend forever,*

*Aurora Middleton*

Wilhelmina wiped away a tear and sniffed. It hurt to know Aurora faced a loveless marriage to the pampered and quite unworthy of her friend, Milford Jameson, a well-known, ruthless rake. She doubted the man would change his ways after marriage. Their father had not set a good example, as the man's escapades were often the talk of the town.

She'd write Aurora right away. If anything, hopefully letters between them would brighten her friend's days. It saddened her to not be in attendance for her best friend's wedding. The nuptials were to take place in February, which was six weeks away.

If only there was a way to help Aurora.

The door swung open and Tobias stood in the opening with an armload of wood. With the sun behind him and the wind blowing his long hair every which way, he looked sort of like a warrior. An angelic one, she'd say.

If Marcus was an attractive man, she could only describe Tobias as magnificent. Quite tall and broad shouldered, he towered over the other men. His clear green eyes contrasted with the dark brown hair and tawny complexion.

He stomped the snow from his boots and walked inside. Wilhelmina rushed to close the door, pulling her shawl tight around her. "It's so windy today."

"It is. But not as cold as it has been."

Shivering, she frowned at her brother-in-law. "How can you possibly tell? It seems the same one day to the next to me."

He shook his head. "Once you've lived her a few years, you'll feel it." While he stacked the wood carefully beside the fireplace, she watched him closely, tapping a finger to her pursed lips.

"Tobias, did you get any replies from the ad Eleanor placed?"

The shrug was noncommittal, so she persisted. "If there are any, weather may have precluded them from arriving."

When he looked over his shoulder at her, his eyes narrowed. "Did Eleanor say something about it?"

"No. I'm just curious. Marcus told me you were building a house as well."

"I'm not in any hurry to get married. Won't bother me in the least if I never do."

"Don't be ridiculous," Eleanor said, walking to her brother and hovering over him. "I need to cut your hair."

"After winter. It keeps my neck warm."

The siblings stared at each other with neither backing down. Wilhelmina chuckled. "I think you should leave it be, Eleanor. Besides, it suits him."

Tobias gave his sister a triumphant look and grinned. "It suits me," he said and straightened to his full height. "Got work to do." With that, he rushed back outside.

Eleanor neared and studied Wilhelmina. "I heard what you talked about. I think Tobias is throwing away any letters that come."

"I may have an idea." Wilhelmina pulled her sister-in-law to the kitchen. "Let's have tea while I explain."

Marcus had pushed his body and, that evening, he could barely stand on his swollen ankle. Wilhelmina held his foot, now across her lap, and rubbed liniment into it. "I will wrap it. In the morning, it will be good as new. You'll see."

Her soft smile melted his insides. For an instant, the pain was forgotten.

"You'll need to stay off of it as much as possible for the next few days."

"There isn't much to do tomorrow. Tobias and I got a lot done today."

Jacob entered the room, his gaze moving across the seated members of the family. Eleanor sat by the fireplace reading, while James looked on. Tobias was at the dining table sketching, as he was prone to do in the evenings now.

"I want to talk to everyone about something," the patriarch announced. At once, every set of eyes moved to Jacob. "I'm thinking I'll move to the smaller house once spring comes. Eleanor, you and James should remain here. I need to get away."

He didn't need to say more, understanding dawned. Although in his late forties, the man remained handsome with only whispers of greying on his temples. Wilhelmina considered that he was much too young to become a recluse and live alone without his family.

Obviously, Eleanor thought the same when exchanging looks with Wilhelmina. "That won't do at all, Pa. I won't have you living alone. If you don't want to stay here, I understand, but wherever you go...we go."

"If Pa's gonna live with anyone, he'll live with Wilhelmina and me." Marcus sat up straighter. Wilhelmina considered tossing his leg off her lap. Once again, he rushed to make a decision without consulting her.

Jacob, obviously the smartest of the group, looked to James and then to Wilhelmina. "Don't you think you should speak to your spouses before offering?"

Eleanor rolled her eyes. "James and I have already spoken about it." She gave Marcus a pointed look and his eyes rounded.

It was comical when he looked at her. "Don't you agree?"

Grief remained in Jacob Hamilton's eyes. A tangible sadness hung on him and Wilhelmina felt sad, too. No one should have to suffer the loss of a wife or husband, especially when so young. It was hard to fathom what she'd do if something happened to Marcus. How could someone overcome such grief?

"I think you are making a decision at a time when it's hard to think clearly. It's understandable that you wish to get away from things that remind you of your wife. However, Mr. Hamilton, I don't think being alone is the answer."

"Come spring, Marcus and I will move out." Wilhelmina looked to her husband. "Of course, you are welcome to move out with us." Marcus blew out a breath of relief.

Jacob scratched his head. "I knew you all would try to talk me out of it." He went to the table and sat down. "I don't plan to become a recluse. But I want each of you to have your own home, a life. I would like it if you all would understand."

Eleanor went to her father and draped her arms around

his shoulders. "I do, Pa. If that's what you want, then you can move into our house. It's the closest. I'll expect you here for supper every night."

Jacob nodded his head. "Agreed."

Tobias scowled. "What about me? I don't want to stay here with you two." He looked to James as if for support.

"You," Eleanor snapped, "will finish your house and move into it. Come spring, we're getting you married."

The youngest raked both hands through his hair and looked up to the ceiling. He remained silent. Eleanor smiled at Wilhelmina. "I have a feeling you'll have a bride sooner than you think."

Tobias jerked upright and looked to Wilhelmina then to his sister. "Why?"

"You'll see." Eleanor kissed her father's temple and went to the kitchen. "Who wants coffee?"


Wilhelmina walked through the darkened house after everyone went to bed. She was restless. Between wondering if she'd been hasty in what she'd proposed to Aurora in her response and trying to figure out if, indeed, she expected a child, her mind would not settle.

She'd not had her monthly courses yet, but the symptoms of a possible pregnancy had disappeared entirely. Each morning, she'd felt well and not at all nauseous or dizzy.

Perhaps it was the many changes in her life that affected her. Once everything settled into a regular routine, her body would react.

Scratching at the kitchen door made her hesitate. When it didn't sound again, she shrugged it off. Probably a branch blown by the wind or a wild animal. Just as she went to leave the room, once again, there were scratches.

Later, she'd consider how foolish she'd been to open the door, as it could have been a man bent on murder. But instead, a small dog stood at the door, her stomach

146

extended with pregnancy. The small creature whined and shivered.

Immediately, Wilhelmina rushed to a side cupboard and pulled out a pair of old tablecloths. Under a small table, she placed a basket with a tablecloth inside of it.

"Come on, girl. It's warm and safe here."

Although timid, it was obvious the dog had been someone's pet by the trust in her eyes. She went to the basket and settled, offering a lick to Wilhelmina's hand in gratitude.

Wilhelmina found leftover roast and potatoes. She cut it up and offered it to the dog, which devoured it all. After setting a dish of water near, she covered the dog, petted its head and made towards her room.

The little dog whined, seeming to be fearful to be left alone.

Wilhelmina wondered if it was about to give birth and was terrified. "Fine, I'll sit with you for a while."

She grabbed a blanket from the main room and returned to the kitchen. Settling in the corner with her back to the wall, she let out a sigh.

"I know how you feel. I came to this house alone and without knowing what awaited me on the other side. It's a safe place. I am accepted and loved. In turn, I've fallen in love with my wonderful husband and care deeply for the rest of the family, too."

The dog watched her as she spoke, its eyes closing from exhaustion.

In the morning, Marcus found his wife sleeping on the floor next to a small dog and three tiny puppies in a basket.

# Chapter Sixteen

*Three weeks later...*

Marcus woke to the sounds of retching. Wilhelmina had been ill in the mornings for three days straight. He lifted from the bed to find her straightening and immediately rinsing out her mouth.

When she turned and grinned at him, he wondered if the woman was feverish. Why would anyone be glad when obviously quite ill?

"Do you need me to get some tea started?" He slid to the edge of the bed. "I can ask Eleanor for something soothing."

He went closer and felt her forehead, finding it cool. His chest tightened. What if what his mother had now affected Wilhelmina. She'd started off by being sick after meals and sometimes in the mornings. He pulled Wilhelmina into his arms to keep her from seeing how distraught he'd suddenly become.

"I'm fine, Marcus. Don't be upset." She pushed back enough to look up at him. "However, I may be ill in the mornings for a few more weeks. It's natural."

"Natural? How can you say that?"

"I'm fairly certain, and Eleanor agrees, that I'm expecting." She blushed. "We're going to have a son or daughter."

Without thinking she'd just been sick, he plucked her from the floor and twirled around and around. "We're going to be parents?" He finally put her down when she turned an interesting shade of green.

Wilhelmina nodded and accepted his kiss. "I would love some tea. Please be a dear and get it while I get dressed."

He rushed from the room and burst into his brother's bedroom. Tobias, who remained in bed, lifted up to his elbows. "What's wrong?"

"Nothing," Marcus replied and grinned down at his brother. "I'm going to be a father."

His brother shook his head and smiled in return. "That's good news. Sure didn't waste any time."

"No, I did not," Marcus said, puffing out his chest. "I'm going to tell Pa." He rushed away.

Everyone hugged a blushing Wilhelmina at breakfast, even James who was not prone to displays of affection.

Marcus couldn't stop grinning even though his cheeks ached from it.


Several days later, the day was sunny, but still quite cold.

James passed a small envelope to Wilhelmina. "Got this yesterday while in town. It's a telegram for you."

Eleanor perked up, her eager gaze on Wilhelmina as she skimmed the contents. She grinned at Eleanor. "Aurora has agreed. I can't believe it."

"Who?" Marcus looked to his wife who continued to exchange curious looks with Eleanor.

"My dearest friend," Wilhelmina said, "is coming here."

She looked to Tobias who'd stopped eating and narrowed his eyes. "She's interesting in pursuing a marriage to Tobias."

Food fell from Tobias' mouth, but he didn't seem to notice. "I'm not interested."

"You will be," Eleanor piped up.

Tobias turned to Jacob. "Pa, tell them they can't go around forcing people to marry each other."

"I think it's a grand idea. There aren't enough women out here and its time you settle down, Tobias."

When he looked to Marcus, there was fear in his gaze. The conversation in the barn returned to his mind. A reminder of how Tobias felt on the matter of marriage.

Tobias stood, grabbed his coat from the peg by the door and went outside.

"Can you speak to him, please?" Wilhelmina touched Marcus' arm. "It won't do if Aurora leaves her home to get away from an unpleasant situation only to find herself in another."

When Marcus caught up with his brother, he found him leaning on a fence peering off into the distance. "It's hard to believe in a few weeks all this will be green again."

"Yeah, I can't wait," Marcus replied and stood next to him. "The one thing that's constant is change."

"I wish the women would stop trying to control our lives." There was a tone of sulkiness to Tobias' statement that reminded Marcus of when his brother was a boy.

"It's how women are. Always romanticizing things."

For a few moments, they remained in companionable silence. Finally, Marcus looked to his brother. "Ma made me promise I'd ensure you are happy. Tell me something. Will you be happy living alone in that house you're building? Is that what you wish for?" He held up a hand so Tobias would not say anything yet.

"If it's what you really want. If you swear it will be a happy life, then I'll tell Wilhelmina to send the woman a telegram right away to tell her not to come."

Tobias scowled. "I don't know what will make me happy."

"You have to tell me, Tobias. I need to know because I

promised our mother and I won't go against it. The day she died, it was one of her last requests. That I ensure you were happy."

His brother's stormy gaze met his. "I don't know what I want right now. I want Ma back. I want things to be as they were when she was healthy."

Marcus put his arm around his brother's shoulders and stood by silently as Tobias cried. It was a relief that he finally grieved.

"Is Tobias all right?" Wilhelmina laid her head on Marcus' shoulder later that night. "He was somber at supper. Do you think he'll reject Aurora?"

"No. I think it could work out. He couldn't admit he'll be happy alone. I promised Ma I'd see to his happiness, so marriage may be good for him."

She let out a sigh and cupped his jaw, turning him to face her. "I love you so much, Marcus. I want Aurora and Tobias to both have something like this."

"So do I. I wish it more than anything for my brother."

He pulled her into his arms and kissed her soundly until both began tearing each other's clothes off.

Along with sighs, moans and kissing, the night sounds of the wind through the trees joined in the simple melody of a good life.

The End

Be sure to read **Aurora, a Romantic Bride** next, you will get to know doctor Evan Jones a lot better!

Sacrifice comes at great cost to a young woman forced to marry and save her family from ruin.

Aurora Middleton loses her best friend and a chance of love at the same time. When confronted with how horrible her life will become, she makes a decision that brings a monumental change. Moving west, leaving all she's ever known will either be a fresh start or the beginning of something worse.

Evan Jones left his life of high society firmly back east. Now the small town doctor has a comfortable life in the Laurel, Montana. When a storm hits, he offers Aurora Middleton and her friend a place to stay all the time resenting the attraction he feels to a woman that reminds him of a life he'd purposely left in the past.

*First Chapter for*

# A ROMANTIC BRIDE

MAIL ORDER BRIDES FOR ALL SEASONS

# HILDIE MCQUEEN

# Chapter One

*Philadelphia, Pennsylvania 1872*

With each click of silverware and every indignant sniff, Aurora became more convinced her decision to run away from it all was the right one.

Mrs. Jameson, her soon to be mother-in-law's calculating gaze shifted to her and Aurora's blood ran cold. What would the dragon expect of her now? Not yet a member of the elite Jameson family and already the burden to become a "pillar" of society grew heavy.

"Aurora, I expect your help in planning the spring ball. It will be our first social event with you as part of the family. We can't disappoint."

Disappoint whom? Every suck up in town would attend and pronounce it the best event ever. Of course, there would be whispers in smaller circles criticizing every detail, from the decorations to the outfits they wore. None, however would openly criticize a member of the Jameson family for fear of being found out and ostracized from society.

Aurora's own closest friend Wilhelmina had been

tarnished and subsequently sent away because of one of the Jameson's.

Assuring a pleasant smile Aurora met the woman's gaze. "Of course." Fortunately her reply was with a much stronger voice than she'd thought possible as mentally she'd already moved away and could care less about any ball or what the people they associated with thought about.

Her family was prominent and included in every guest list in the area. Not because they had a lot of money, but mainly because of her father's title. His aristocratic lineage was of high value and since Aurora was the eldest of the only two daughters, whoever married her would be the next Duke of Edenton.

Her mother, who constantly fawned over Mrs. Jameson, for whatever reason smiled primly. "Of course both of us will help. Anything you need, all you have to do is ask. It's such a wonderful thing for our two families to join."

Ever since Aurora had become engaged to Milford Jameson, one would think it was her mother who wore the five-carat monstrosity weighing Aurora's left hand. Her mother constantly fell over backwards to accommodate any request by the Jameson's, especially the matriarch.

Her father on the other hand, was the opposite, expecting everyone else for the most part to direct his social life. If left to his own, he'd remain in his study reading and scribbling ideas about social economic findings. Not surprisingly, he had little to say on the marriage and for that Aurora was grateful. He listened to her lament on the idea of marrying someone she didn't love with a gentle pat on the shoulder.

Once in a while when she'd asked if there was a way out of the predicament, he'd comment. "We all have to do what is expected," which of course didn't help her feel any better.

This night her father was much more interested in the lively conversation with the male in attendance on the expansion of the railroad towards the northwest interjecting he'd known all along it would be a good investment eventually.

The damned railroad was the main reason Aurora found herself in the dreadful situation of marrying the stone-faced man who's calculating gaze met hers every so often. A constant reminder of what he'd told her to expect after the meal.

He demanded she allow him more access to her body. Not quite so far as to take her virginity, for he pronounced he'd not pursue full intimacy until after the wedding, but enough to satisfy him. Whatever that meant.

Although he was not unattractive and power did add appeal to Milford Jameson, it was his demeanor that she found unpleasant. He rarely smiled and usually kept his eyes half closed, as if bored and his voice, it irritated her so much.

When he spoke, instead of a deep masculine sound, it was shrill, a higher pitch then one would expect from a man. Silly things Aurora found annoying, probably because of the forced marriage to him.

She pushed food around on her plate, her appetite gone once the reminder of Milford doing who knew what to her struck. She slid a glance to her father and considered feigning illness.

Her plan was in place to leave Philadelphia. She'd stolen away items to a cousin's house one bag load at a time, then later, using the excuse of gifting Esther clothing, she'd taken dresses and shoes.

Thank God she could rely on her wonderful cousin. Esther was a beautiful vibrant woman, who understood Aurora's situation perfectly. Just seven years earlier at the tender age of sixteen her cousin was married to a much older man in her family's effort to gain social standing.

The man had turned out to be a miserly sort who doled out just enough money to barely pay for necessities. As a result, although her sisters had gained invitations to social affairs, Esther had never set foot at social events again. Her clothing became dull and old since her husband refused to pay for new clothing, claiming she already owned too many.

Thanks to Esther's marriage, her family's gain had been the demise of her otherwise happy life. In spite of her situation, Esther became industrious in finding ways around her husband's stinginess and had developed beautiful soap making skills. The sales of her soaps brought her income, which she saved and used to purchase small necessities.

Aurora shivered at the thought that although the Jameson's would most definitely ensure she maintained an up to date wardrobe, like Esther, she'd give up happiness in exchange for marriage.

The entire engagement had come to be quite unexpectedly, to Aurora anyway. She'd been forced into the marriage when her father's investment of the entire family fortune was lost on a railroad venture.

Now just a few short month's later, his investment had paid off and her family was once again wealthy. However, it was too late for her and afraid to lose social status, her parents could never request the retraction of the engagement.

Of course the Jameson's had jumped on the opportunity to gain a title for their eldest son, Milford, who'd pronounced Aurora to be an attractive woman who'd fit perfectly in the role of his wife.

Role indeed, she mentally kicked him under the table.

When Milford's startled gaze met hers, she gasped. "Sorry, my leg cramped," Aurora fought not to giggle at having actually kicked him.

"Are you unwell? You haven't touched your food. Excited about something perhaps?" His attempt at humor only made her want to throw up the little food she had eaten.

"I am a bit uneasy tonight. Something didn't quite sit

well with me," Aurora replied with a pointed look satisfied at noting the tight lines around her intended's mouth.

"I'm sure you'll feel better later." He looked away, dismissing her for the moment.

Aurora looked around the table. With painted on smiles and nods at whatever boring dribble the person next to them said, it was evident the only person enjoying the evening was her father. The triumphant air at no longer being financially dependent on the Jameson's had him positively glowing.

She loved the often-distracted man like no one else. From his crooked spectacles, to the unruly mop of hair and lopsided cravat, he never pretended to be anyone special. Yet he had the title, the one thing every one of the pretentious people around the table coveted.

As the meal finally ended and people congregated in circles to drink and continue conversing, Aurora fortified herself for time alone with Milford.

"Oh my goodness!" someone cried out as her soon to be mother in law fell limp to the floor. The matriarch, who was not above theatrics to get attention, or ensure there was some sort of talk of the dinner afterwards lay on the thick carpet in a perfect pose ensuring her face was dramatically full of despair.

Milford, his brother Earnest and the husband rushed to her side as she lifted a hand to her brow.

"Darling, let us help you to the bedroom. You must have over taxed yourself tonight," Mr. Jameson exclaimed, his gaze meeting someone's across the room. Aurora followed his line of sight.

Gertrude Mansfield's, a woman Aurora heard was the man's latest lover, met his gaze and her lips curved as if holding back a secret while she watched the drama unfold.

Women coo'ed at Milford's mother as he and his father helped her to the stairway, and not a second later they moved away and reached for a fresh cocktail. It was well understood. They were to remain until Mr. Jameson returned to give an update on his wife's health.

The conversation buzzed as Aurora moved closer to the patio doorway.

"I hope you are paying attention to your mother in law's lessons on how to keep your social events forefront on society's lips." The woman, Gertrude had come to stand next to her.

She was pretty in a no-nonsense sort of way, her dark hair pulled up into a tumble of curls. Gertrude rolled her eyes and curled her upper lip. "All she had to do was feign a headache and excuse herself if she was bored of our company. Of course that would not have made for gossip fodder."

"It does cut our evening short, which is distressful for some of the guests. This way she cannot be blamed." Aurora said immediately regretting her slip. "However, I'm sure she overtaxed herself today."

The woman smiled and Aurora immediately liked her. "Perhaps this is a good time for me to slip away. I find myself with a headache."

Gertrude lifted an eyebrow. "I can certainly understand why."

Not wanting to ponder what Gertrude knew, Aurora nodded and hurried away.

She went to her father, who stood next to doors leading outside through the gardens. "Enjoy the rest of your evening father. I'm going home. I have a headache."

He looked around the room and huffed. "Quite so. I'll join you." He motioned for her mother who shook her head. "Ah well, she'll ride home with the Patterson's I'm sure as she will remain until the end to ensure our hostess is not in grave danger of sudden death." He mumbled and Aurora laughed gaining astonished looks.

"Come Father before you get me in more trouble."

*Aurora* is available now!

*Two Other Stories I know you'll enjoy!*

## Beneath a Silver Sky

What happens with a young woman's first love is a hardened man?

Trouble follows Brogan Hage into Silver City, Idaho, when injuries force him to seek medical attention. An unexpected offer has him thinking about settling in the bustling town. Between outlaws showing up and a beautiful passionate woman, the hardened lawman is not sure which is more dangerous.

Town doctor's daughter, Sarah Sutherland, finds herself fiercely attracted to the wounded U.S. Marshal in her care. The fact he has a reputation for ruthlessness does not stop her from falling in love.

## Under a Silver Moon

Lucas McKade and Camille Johnston, attempt to leave the past behind only to find true happiness, comes only they face it. The shadows of the past fall over Silver City, Idaho casting its darkness over a man and a woman attempting to start anew.

When US Marshal Lucas McKade, new deputy of Silver City, Idaho decided to settle down, he didn't consider bringing complications to the town. Against every instinct he seeks out apothecary owner Camille Johnston, a woman who calls to his basic nature to protect and to make his.

Camille knows that eventually the secrets of her past will come to haunt, yet she hopes to keep things hidden as long as possible and enjoy her lonely but peaceful existence in Silver City. The new deputy brings with him desires she'd thought firmly shut away. A relationship of any kind would mean dangerous consequences.

# About the Author

*Whether a rancher, a highlander or a hunky cowboy, you will fall in love with Hildie McQueen's heroes!*

Hello Dear Reader. Writing is my dream come true. There is nothing I love more than bringing my characters and stories to life and sharing them with you.

I thoroughly loved writing Wilhelmina and Marcus' story. If you enjoyed Wilhelmina, A Winter Bride, please recommend it to your friends and family and leave me a review.

I love hearing from my readers and am always excited when you join my newsletter to keep abreast of new releases and other things happening in my world. Newsletter sign up: http://goo.gl/PH6Doo

Other Hildie McQueen Links:

Website: http://www.HildieMcQueen.com

Facebook: http://www.facebook.com/HildieMcQueen

Twitter: https://twitter.com/HildieMcQueen

Instagram: @HildieWrites

I answer all emails: Hildie@HildieMcQueen.com

HILDIE McQUEEN
ENTICING. ENGAGING. ROMANCE.